BURNING MEMORIES

By

Paula K. Kohl

ISBN: 1-4107-2902-8 (e-book)
ISBN: 1-4107-2901-X (Paperback)
ISBN: 1-4107-2900-1 (Dust Jacket)

Library of Congress Control Number: 2003091399

This book is printed on acid free paper.

Printed in the United States of America
Bloomington, IN

1stBooks - rev. 10/29/03

This book is dedicated to my loving husband Jerome.
Without his encouragement and gentle urgings
to never lose sight of my dream, this
book would not have been possible.

Chapter One

Andrea sat starring out at her family's enormous cherry orchard from her bedroom window. It was all she could see for miles and miles. I'm glad to be back home, she thought. Being away at college was fun, but it's still nice to come home. All I know is that I'm glad I have only one more year to go. Hopefully, things will be different when I go back in the fall.

After a while she decided to go to see what her parents were doing and she knew just where to find them. Every evening, you could find them setting on their front porch enjoying the view. Perched high above Lake Michigan, Cherry Wood Mansion has a fabulous view of the setting sun. Watching sunsets is one of her parents' favorite things to do. Lake Michigan sunsets are beautiful and romantic and her parents were incurable romantics.

As Andrea neared the porch, she could hear her parents gently teasing each other. Everyone who came in contact with her parents realized just how much in love they were. This was very comforting to Andrea. It provided her with a sense of feeling safe and secure. No matter what was going on in her parents' life, they always managed to find time for each other. Whether it was watching the sunset or just spending a few quiet moments alone, they never let a day go by without spending time together.

Andrea opened the door to the porch and said, "Another beautiful evening and no clouds blocking the sunset?

"It sure is. I never get tired of watching it," Andrea's mother, Shirley said.

"Me either," her father Tom said as he hugged Shirley.

"You two are something else" Andrea teased.

1

"We know," Tom said smiling.

"Andrea will you be able to help me in the Flower Shop tomorrow?" Shirley asked. "Sara needs to take the day off and the shop has been very busy lately with all the summer tourists' back in town. I could really use the help."

Andrea's mother ran the local Flower Shop purely as a hobby. It wasn't necessary for her to have a job. Shirley and Tom Higgins were very wealthy. They owned the Lake View Cherry Orchard. Lake View Cherry Orchard is the largest cherry orchard in Michigan. The Higgins' family is well known in this part of the state and is synonymous with wealth and power. Shirley didn't need to work. She just enjoyed working.

"I already have plans for tomorrow," Andrea said. Though her only plans were to stay as close to home as possible. At home she felt safe.

"Whatever you have planned for tomorrow will just have to wait," Tom said. "If your mother needs your help, you're going to help."

Andrea tried to think of a way out of helping her mother but couldn't come up with one. She finally agreed "Oh alright." Then turned and headed back in the house and to her bedroom.

Andrea began recalling the events that had happened at college over the last year. Andrea was quite popular with her classmates. She had brought some of her friends' home over Christmas in prior years, but not this past year. She asked friends to visit during the summer in prior years, but again not this year.

Andrea always had lots of dates but no steady beau. Young men tried their best to get her interested in them, but none of them were able to capture her heart. Andrea was not only beautiful; she was also rich. That was a combination most men would do just about anything for and Andrea knew it. She was very careful regarding men's intentions. Were they sincere or were they just after her money? She considered all the young men she dated as nothing more than a friend and always appeared a little aloof to them. Young and old men alike flocked to her side when she entered a room. It seemed men always paid attention to her, but she was not intrigued by any of them, except one.

This past year at college, a certain young man had become obsessed with her. He focused all of his energy trying to get her interested in him. Try as hard as she could, Andrea was unsuccessful in dissuading his interest. Andrea didn't want him to get interested in her for a number of good reasons.

His name is Alex Longred and he's the leader of the Black Claw Gang. Alex wasn't bad looking. In fact, he appeared capable of being quite good looking, but due to the way he lived and dressed, he always looked and was filthy. Possibly, just possibly, underneath all that filth could be the makings of a very handsome man, but no woman wanted to find out.

He and his gang were well known on campus for their notorious actions. When they decided they wanted something, they let nothing get in their way. The police tried many times to jail all of the gang and put them away forever. Because Alex's uncle Lance is a very prominent lawyer who specializes in criminal defense, they managed to get off on minor technicalities. It didn't matter to him if they actually committed the crimes or not.

Shirley and Tom were talking as they headed towards their bedroom for the night.

"I wonder what seems to be bothering Andrea lately? She's been acting very strange since she got home from college. She hasn't talked much about college either. She almost acts as if she's scared of something," Shirley said.

"I know, and I don't understand it myself," Tom added. "She's been sticking awfully close to home too. Maybe I should have a talk with her."

"No, I don't think that will help. Besides, I've already tried to prod her along to talk to me with little success. You know how stubborn she can be. She isn't about to admit it even if she is scared or upset about something. She's always been too proud to admit any weaknesses. I wish she wasn't quite so independent," Shirley added.

"Maybe she's just having trouble adjusting to being home after living away at college for the last three years and being on her own."

"All in all, if she doesn't start acting better soon, I think I'll have Jason talk with her. He seems to have more luck getting her to open up and talk about what's bothering her then we do," Tom added as they continued up the stairs.

Jason. He was the one man who managed to stir Andrea's feelings. Jason had worked for the family doing odd jobs around the orchard as young boy. When he got older Tom trusted him enough to put him in charge of one of the largest sections of their cherry orchard. Jason's parents had worked for the Higgins family for years before they were killed in a car accident. Mr. & Mrs. Higgins took Jason in and cared for him until he was old enough to live on his own. Then he moved into the cottage house next to Cherry Wood Mansion. Jason was always Andrea's escort to the many social functions the family attended. He easily fell into the role of Andrea's guardian as she grew up. Andrea had two older brothers; Daniel and George.

The Lake View Cherry Orchard is located in the Leelanau Peninsula in northern Michigan. When Tom's father passed away, Tom inherited the orchards. Tom's father, Harold and his wife, Sara, came north in search of a better life. After exploring a few different areas of Michigan, they settled in the northwest corner of northern Michigan's lower peninsula commonly referred to as the little finger of Michigan. They had brought with them their meager savings in hopes of being able to purchase land. Land at this time in northwest Michigan was relatively inexpensive. Harold and Sara were able to purchase 20 acres.

For the first few years they experimented with different types of crops. They tried planting potatoes, corn, cherry trees, beets, and wheat. After about ten years of experimenting they determined that growing cherries was the most profitable. The climate in this area of Michigan is perfect for growing cherries. The peninsula has Lake Michigan on one side and Grand Traverse Bay on the other. Surrounded by these waters, the summers are tempered from getting too hot and winters' insulating blanket of snow keeps it from getting too cold. The lakes provide ample moisture in the summer and winter for the cherry trees. Soon Harold was boasting of a bumper crop of cherries. After each summer's harvest, he bought more and more acreage until he had acquired 3,000 acres of prime cherry growing land. This made the Higgins family the largest cherry farmer's in the state. This land was not only good for cherries but, remarkably beautiful. Their orchard consists of acres of rolling hills, woods, a small creek, magnificent views of Lake Michigan to the west, the Sleeping Bear Sand Dunes to the south, and Grand Traverse Bay in the east. The view of these lakes was how the name of Lake View Cherry Orchard came about. His father eventually built a huge mansion called 'Cherry Wood' on their property. This is where the Higgins family still lives. Harold and Sara had two children, a son named Tom, and a daughter named Sandra.

Jason was widely known in the area and respected by everyone, including the Higgins family. His muscular frame, finely chiseled face, blue eyes, dark brown hair and elegant manners made most women stare in awe at him. Jason enjoyed working for the Higgins family very much, especially when he was called upon to escort Andrea.

Andrea was lying on her bed crying when she heard her parents coming up the stairs to go to bed for the night. She quieted her sobs as they passed by her room. She didn't want them to hear her.

She didn't want to leave her house the next day nor work in her mother's Flower Shop. She wasn't sure if Alex knew where she lived but she didn't want to go out in public for fear of running into him. On her last day of college he had asked her once again to go out with him. She immediately declined and stated that there was no way she would ever go out with him.

He grabbed her wrists, pulled her towards him and said, "Andrea darling, if you say no, I'm afraid I'll be forced to use this on that pretty face of yours. If you tell me no again, I'll leave you scarred for life."

Alex had pulled a knife out of his jacket and was holding it under her chin. "When I'm finished with you and your family, you'll wish you were dead too." His eyes seemed to brighten with fire as he finished talking to her. She finally agreed to go out with him over the summer and he let go of her. She quickly walked away without having told him where she lived. She knew it was just a matter of time before he figured out where the Lake View Cherry Orchard was. It was well known at her college that she was the daughter of the wealthy owner of the Lake View Cherry Orchard. She knew he would eventually come for her. When he did, she had to be ready with a way of getting out of the date. Hopefully, in a way that he'd accept and not harm her or her family. That feat seemed next to impossible.

She didn't know what he might do. After all, he said that she'd wish she were dead too. What did he mean by that? Would he cause her family harm or just her? Did he mean he'd kill her family but leave her alive? He wouldn't really hurt her family just because she wouldn't go out with him on date. Or would he? When the time came, how was she going to get out of this mess?

Andrea finally stopped crying and walking over to her mirror, she studied herself carefully then stated out loud, "I'm not going to let him or anyone else scare me into doing something I don't want to do. I'm a grown woman who can manage her own life. I'm afraid of no one." She put on her nightgown and went to bed. In her heart, however, she knew that Alex was more then she would be able to deal with all by herself. Sleep was not long in coming since she was exhausted from trying to deal with her situation.

Jason got up early and decided to join the Higgins family for breakfast. Normally he didn't join them for breakfast but for some reason he felt compelled to join them today. Entering the kitchen he saw the whole family sitting at the table except for Andrea. It looked like a typical morning at the Higgins house. Marabel, the cook, was serving breakfast and Tom was sitting in his usual chair reading the morning newspaper.

"Good morning Jason," Shirley said. "Nice to have you join us this morning. You know you really should eat breakfast with us more often. I know that when you don't eat with us, you usually don't have any breakfast and that's not good for you."

Jason sat down. "Good morning to you too." He said as he smiled at her. His smile told her that he appreciated her concern about his eating habits, but he wasn't about to change.

Andrea walked in relieving Jason of having to reply to Shirley's little talk.

"Morning mom, dad, Jason" Andrea said as she sat down and nodded to her brothers as a way of saying good morning.

"Morning sweetheart" Shirley said. After a few moments of silence she added "I think Jason should drive you down to the Flower Shop today when you're ready. It looks like rain out there." Shirley turned towards Jason, "That is, of course, if that won't interfere with any of your plans."

"I'd be happy to," Jason said looking over towards Andrea.

Shirley sighed with relief. She was really concerned about the way Andrea was acting lately and she wanted to be sure that Andrea made it to the Flower Shop today. With Jason driving her she knew Andrea wouldn't be able to make up an excuse not to show up.

"Fine with me" Andrea said "I didn't feel like hurrying to get ready to go with you this morning anyway. I'd probably make you late in opening up the shop." At least this way she would be able to stall leaving the house for a little longer. With Jason driving her, the chances of running into Alex on the way would be slim. Finishing her breakfast she headed back upstairs to get ready.

Taking as much time as she dared, she finally went outside to find Jason. She knew she couldn't waste anymore time. She found him by the main orchard barn working on a piece of machinery used for harvesting cherries.

"Hi Jason" Andrea said. "I guess I'm ready now."

"Okay. Just give me a minute to make one last adjustment," he said. "Go ahead and get in the car. I'll be right there." Andrea headed toward Jason's car.

As Jason got in he asked "So I bet you've got big plans for the upcoming weekend right?"

"No. I wasn't planning on doing much of anything," Andrea said flatly.

"I thought your weekend would be all booked up since you haven't done anything since you got home. That's not like you Andrea. What's up?"

"Nothing! Nothing at all!" she yelled.

They drove the rest of the way in silence. Something was really troubling her. He'd seen it in the way she'd

8

been acting and her response to his question confirmed it. He had heard her parents talking about it too. None of them had been able to figure out what it was. She's such a proud young lady, and things rarely get her down, or at least she was always too proud to show it. Jason's concern grew even stronger as he watched Andrea's face turn pale white as they passed a blue metallic van. She stared at the van as they drove by it.

"Andrea, what's the matter? You're as white as a ghost?" he asked with much concern.

Andrea mumbled under her breath "Help, please help me."

Finally she said out loud "Why nothing" as they pulled up in front of the Flower Shop. She jumped out of the car and slammed the door shut before Jason could say another word.

He had heard only one little 'help' and he didn't understand. What in the world could possibly trouble her to the point that she'd need help from him, but be too afraid to ask him for it. His heart went out to her. He loved Andrea very much and hoped that someday she would be his wife. After all, she had just turned twenty-two. He was thirty. That wasn't too much of an age difference. Age didn't matter anyway. What mattered was if you loved each other. Love . . . that was the problem. He knew she loved him, but only like a big brother. Would she ever be able to love him as a wife loves a husband? Someday, somehow he would see to it that she did. He continued watching her walk into the shop. He wanted to run after her and protect her from whatever it was she was so afraid of, but he knew he couldn't do that. After waiting and watching for a while, he turned the car around and left. In the back of his mind he kept thinking of the blue metallic van. Why had she reacted so when she saw it? Who was in that van and what did it have to do with her?

Andrea entered the Flower Shop and in looking around realized that everything was all right. Alex was nowhere in sight so he hadn't seen her as they drove past him. Her mother waved to her from behind the counter.

"It's a good thing you finally got here. I need to fill all of these orders," she said as she held up a stack of papers. "We've had a steady stream of customers this morning so I haven't been able to work on any of them. I'll need you to manage the floor while I work in the back."

"Okay" Andrea said.

She was positive it had been Alex Longred in that van. No one else drove a van that color. She hadn't talked much at college about her mother running a Flower Shop so she doubted he'd know to look for her here. But she knew it wouldn't take him long to figure out where she lived. All he had to do was ask around town where the Higgins family lived and he'd be directed to it. Hopefully, he'd stop by her house and when he finds out I'm not there he'll go away, but probably not. Mostly likely he'd ask where she was. If Marabel answered the door she wouldn't tell him but if one of her brothers answered the door they'd tell him. If Marabel didn't tell him he'd just come back over and over again until she was at home. She didn't dare tell her family about him. They'd ask too many questions and he just might go through with his threat to harm her family.

Customers were flocking into the shop. This helped take her mind off Alex. She couldn't believe how many people kept coming in. She was so busy she hadn't noticed a group of her old high school girl friends come in.

Finally Sue said, "Hey Andrea aren't you going to say hi to us?"

Andrea looked up. A big smile broke across her face as she saw her best friend from high school, Sue, standing there with three of her other girl friends Mary, Paige and Linda.

"Hello you guys," she said as she came out from behind the counter and gave each of them a big hug. "It's so great to see you."

"You too" Linda said.

"How long have you been home?" Paige asked.

"About two weeks," she answered.

"So what have you been doing? Why didn't you let us know you were home?" Sue asked.

"I've been busy with family things," Andrea responded.

"Too busy for a quick phone call?" Sue asked smiling.

"You know how it is" Andrea replied.

"Yeah I do" Sue said.

"The last time I talked with you about college, you were worried about some problems with a guy named . . . Alex I think. How'd everything turn out?" Sue asked.

Andrea quickly said "Don't bring him up here. I don't want mom to know anything about him. He's still somewhat of a problem but I'm dealing with it."

"He sounded pretty spooky to me. You know this state has a stalker law. Don't be afraid to use it" Sue said.

"It hasn't gone that far," Andrea said. "Well I've got to get back to work. There are customers lining up."

"Okay" Linda said. "We'll give you a call later and maybe we can get together this weekend."

"Okay. I'll see" Andrea stated as the girls left the shop.

The day was going by so fast. Andrea was kept busy and didn't have time to think about Alex.

Alex was determined to find Andrea. He knew she had purposely said she would go out with him this summer hoping he didn't know where she lived. I'll find out where she lives and walk right up to her front door, he thought. He had heard some of their classmates talking about the Lake View Cherry Orchard so he assumed that was where she lived. He knew she talked about going up

11

north to go home. Alex wasn't a scholar but he knew that in Michigan all the large cherry orchards were around Traverse City. All he had to do was go there and look for the Lake View Cherry Orchard.

He and his gang arrived in Traverse City and stopped at one of the local restaurants for a bite to eat. As they were leaving, low and behold there in a rack next to the door was a pamphlet talking about cherry orchard tours in the area. One of the orchards on the list to tour was the Lake View Cherry Orchard. It provided directions on how to get to there, along with of schedule of the tour times.

"Look here guys" Alex stated as he looked over the pamphlet. "This is just what we needed." Alex added as he pointed to the map on the pamphlet. "Let's get moving" he stated as they climbed into the van and drove towards the orchard.

While Jason was working in the central orchard barn, his mind kept wandering back to Andrea and her reaction to that van. He wanted to go to the Flower Shop to check on her but he couldn't come up with a reason to. After working a while longer and looking at his watch and he realized it was early afternoon and he hadn't had any lunch. Figuring Shirley and Andrea hadn't eaten either he headed towards the kitchen and asked Marabel if she would pack a lunch for him to take to them. Marabel thought it was good idea so she quickly packed some cold chicken and vegetables and then he drove to the Flower Shop.

"Hi" Jason said walking in. "I thought the two of you might be getting hungry so I asked Marabel to pack you a lunch. Here it is."

"That's so nice of you" Andrea said. "Mom, Jason's here with some lunch for us."

Jason headed towards the back room where Shirley was busy putting orders together and Andrea followed him. The steady stream of customers had slowed down to a trickle. Sitting at a table where they could see the front door if anyone walked in they began to eat. Neither of them realized just how hungry they were until they started to eat.

"Jason there's plenty here, please join us," Shirley said.

"Thanks, I think I will" he said sitting down next to Andrea. She seemed much calmer than she had when she got out of his car this morning.

"Everything going okay here?" Jason asked looking directly at Andrea.

Andrea knew he was referring to the way she'd acted this morning. She silently prayed he wouldn't say anything in front of her mother. He didn't and her mother thought he was referring to how the business was going.

"Things seem to be slowing down a little now. I'm close to having all the orders filled and ready to be picked up" Shirley indicated.

The front door opened and a group of ladies entered in the store. Andrea got up and went out to help them. After that, more customers kept coming in keeping Andrea busy.

"Well, I guess I'll go" Jason said to Shirley. "Unless you need me to help you out here?" he asked, secretly hoping she would need his help so he could keep an eye on Andrea.

"No, I think I have everything under control" she said.

"Okay. See you later" Jason said getting up to leave.

As he walked out to the customer floor he watched Andrea for a few minutes. He wanted to catch her eye before he left. Finally she looked up. He mouthed goodbye. She smiled back at him and said goodbye. Then went back to helping her customers as he headed out the door.

That smile, Jason thought, God how that smile gets to me. I want to take her in my arms and then he let his mind wander for a moment. He shook his head, no, no, he thought, not yet. He knew the timing wasn't right for him to make a move on Andrea. He didn't know when, or if that moment would come. He headed back to Cherry Wood Manor.

As Alex and his gang pulled up in front of the Higgins house they were amazed at the size of Cherry Wood Manor.

"Wow!" Ed said. "This place is really something. They have got to be really rich."

"It's amazing" Dick said. "This place must be big enough for five families to live."

Alex acted unimpressed. He got out of the van and went to the door. As he knocked, Daniel answered the door.

"Is Andrea here?" Alex asked.

"Ah, no she isn't" Daniel said.

"Well do you know where she is?" Alex asked.

"I might, but who are you?" Daniel asked.

"My name is Alex. I'm a friend of hers from college. She told me if I was ever in the Traverse City area I should stop by and see her," Alex said.

Daniel didn't think he looked like someone Andrea would spend time with. He smelled and he acted strange. After studying him for a minute he decided he had no real reason not to tell him where Andrea was.

"She's working at our Flower Shop in town. If you go back to Traverse City and go to Front Street. That's one block back from the water. Once you're on Front Street you can't miss it." Daniel said.

"Thanks" Alex said heading back to the van.

Daniel watched him get back in the van and start talking with his buddies. It appeared to be some college guys on a road trip. Still he watched the van until it disappeared.

As Jason was driving home, he saw the blue metallic van pulling out of the Higgin's driveway. Slowing down he watched the van as it went by. He knew it was the same van he and Andrea had passed earlier. He saw a young man driving the van and another one sitting on the passenger side. He watched the van until it was out of sight and then headed to the house. As he got there he saw Daniel standing on the front porch.

"Who was in that van?" Jason asked.

"Some guy named Alex" Daniel said.

"What'd he want?" Jason inquired.

"He was looking for Andrea. He said he was a friend of hers from college so I told him where she was" Daniel said.

"Did he say anything else?" Jason asked impatiently.

"Nope" Daniel added.

When Andrea saw that van this morning it had really upset her, he thought. I wonder if I should go back to the Flower Shop to see if this guy's there and what he wants with Andrea. He finally decided he wouldn't go back. If there was a problem he knew they'd give him or Tom a call. He went back to work.

"Here's Front Street boys," Alex said. "Now look for a Flower Shop."

"There it is" Ed said pointing straight ahead.

Alex pulled the van into the first open parking space he could find.

"I'll be back soon guys," Alex said getting out and heading toward the Flower Shop. Walking in he looked around and saw Andrea behind the cash register. He walked up to her.

"Hello Andrea" Alex said.

Andrea looked up and immediately gasped.

15

He got the reaction he'd expected. She thought he wouldn't be able to find her. At least not so soon.

"Expecting me?" he asked smirking at her.

"Alex, what are you doing here?" she asked trying to remain calm.

"I came to take you out on our date" he stated.

"I, I, I can't go now. I have to work for mom. She's short handed in the store today" Andrea stated.

Shirley came out from the back room in time to hear Andrea say she couldn't go out with him because she was working.

"Andrea" Shirley said "I only need you until closing time. After that you're free aren't you?" Shirley was standing too far back in the shop to get a good look at Alex. If she had, she might have understood Andrea's hesitation.

"No mom. I made plans with the girls for tonight" Andrea said nervously.

Shirley didn't know who Alex was but if he was asking her to go out on a date she was going to encourage Andrea to go. She was staying in the house too much lately. Shirley assumed that she really didn't have any plans for the night. She just wanted to stay in.

"Great. I'll pick you up then. What time do you close?" Alex asked.

"On weekdays usually around 7:00" Shirley stated.

"See you then" Alex said smugly. He walked to the door, stopped and turned back looking at Andrea with that smug look on his face waved goodbye and left.

Andrea just stood there. She couldn't believe her mother was making her go out with Alex. If she only knew what she was doing.

"Mom. I, I . . ." Andrea stopped not finishing her sentence.

"What?" her mother asked.

"Nothing" she said as she tried to go back to work knowing she couldn't tell her mother about Alex and

16

what he was. She'd make a scene, call the police and she still wasn't sure what Alex would do to her family. She would protect them at all costs. Maybe between now and closing time I can come up with some way of getting out of this. She needed time to think.

Jason finished his work, cleaned up and was ready to leave to pick up his girl friend Cindy. Jason thought about Cindy. She was pretty. Cute, in fact, but he was deeply in love with Andrea. He was dating Cindy until he felt the time was right to let Andrea know just how much he loved her. Cindy's blonde hair and blue eyes just didn't do to him what Andrea's beautiful long brown hair and hazel eyes did. Someday Andrea will see me as the man I am, not just as her big brother. He hoped. Jason was well aware of the fact that Cindy always hoped that one day they would get married and how extremely jealous of Andrea she was. He needed to handle Cindy very carefully. He didn't want to crush her when the day came that Andrea finally decided she wanted him, because he truly loved Andrea.

Jason was supposed to pick up Cindy around 7:15, so on his way he decided to drive past the Flower Shop to make sure everything was alright. Driving by slowly he hoped to see Andrea through the window. Sure enough, there she was behind the cash register and appeared to be fine. Everything must be all right, he thought.

Driving on he began thinking about his past and how lucky he was that the Higgins family had taken him in after he lost his parents in a car accident when he was only twelve. They were good to him. To him they were just like his own family. Jason had watched Andrea grow up and turn into a beautiful, sensual woman. He thought back to when he first came to live with the Higgins family. She was so little then, but even then she had managed to capture his attention. He always enjoyed playing with her or escorting her to a party at the tender

17

age of ten. Her parents insisted she attend the many social functions that the family was invited too. She complained about having to act like a lady, but she never seemed to have to act, it came naturally for her.

He had fallen in love with her quite sometime ago. When it actually happened he didn't know, but he was glad it had. Someday he wanted to make her a very real part of his own family. He knew that he was well respected in town, but was he good enough for her? Would the Higgins family allow him to marry her, he wondered? Why think about such things now? She doesn't think of me in that way. She only sees me as a big brother, some one who has the responsibility to protect her and watch over her, which, at times, she really resented and he knew it. She could be so stubborn and once she got something in her head, she usually won no matter what it was. Someday though, he'd get her to see him as a man, but for now he'd just have to wait. The right time would come, but how long, just how long would he have to wait?

Jason pulled into Cindy's drive and slowly walked to the door.

"Hi sweetheart!" Jason said seeing Cindy as she was opening the door. Putting his arms around her he kissed her.

Cindy lovingly returned his kiss and then stepped back staring into his eyes. He was so handsome and those eyes, ah . . . those eyes. They could immobilize you when they looked deep into you.

"Where are we going?" Cindy asked.

"I thought we'd go to the drive-in in Honor" Jason said.

"Well I'm ready on time for a change so let's go."

"Certainly madam" Jason said bowing low as if she was a grand lady of high society. Cindy smiled and they walked to his car. Jason opened her door for her and then he got in.

"What movie is playing?" she asked.

"Chariots of Fire. Is that alright with you?" Jason asked.

"Of course, I'd enjoy any movie as long as I'm with you." She hoped to not see much of the movie anyway.

"Why thank you." Why is she always so easy when she's with me. I sometimes wonder what she's like when she goes out with other men. Is she as easy with them? I really wish she wasn't so eager.

It didn't take too long to get to the drive-in. Jason pulled in and parked close to the back. He wanted to be alone with Cindy, or at least as alone as you can be at a drive-in.

Andrea was watching the clock. It was almost 7:30 and Alex would be arriving any minute and she still hadn't come up with an excuse to get out of going with him.

She almost fainted when Alex walked in. Now she was going to have to go with him. Shirley heard the door open and figured it was the young man coming to pick up Andrea. She looked from around the back and sure enough it was him. She came out to tell them to have a good time.

"Are you all set to go Andrea?" her mother asked.

"Mom are you sure you don't need me to stay and help you close up the shop?" Andrea asked hoping her mother would get the hint that she didn't want to go with Alex, yet not showing her fear.

"No, No, you go ahead. I'll be just fine," she said lightly pushing Andrea towards the door. "You guys go and have a good time. By the way, what are your plans for tonight?"

"I thought we'd go to the drive-in" Alex said. "Grab your coat and let's get going."

Andrea almost fainted at his touch. The thought of having to be alone with him at a drive-in was almost more than she could handle. Try to act as normal as possible she thought. I can't tell mom I don't want to go out with him. He'd just make me go with him now anyway.

As she grabbed her coat Alex said "Let's go."

"Have fun" Shirley said.

"I'm sure we will. I'm sure we will," he added again looking lustfully at Andrea.

Shirley watched as they both walked out of the store. She could tell Andrea was reluctant to go and wondered why. As she continued to watch them she thought there was something awfully familiar about him but she couldn't figure out what it was. He reminded her of someone but she couldn't place who it was. That's funny she thought, Andrea never told me his name. Hopefully, with whatever has been bothering her, going out would do her good. She was sure Andrea had forgotten to introduce him because of the way she'd been acting lately. Then she started closing the shop and reconciling the cash register.

Andrea reluctantly got into Alex's van. Fear was consuming her. She'd heard of the terrible things Alex did to his dates and she was very worried. How am I ever going to get away from him? How do I avoid his advances?

Alex didn't say anything as pulled out onto the street and headed towards the drive-in. As they neared the drive-in he asked, "Why so quiet Andrea? Are you afraid of me?"

Andrea sat in silence.

"You know giving me the silent treatment isn't going to do you any good" he stated. "I've finally got you right where I want you."

That's what she was afraid of. He had the upper hand and she couldn't do anything about it. Where was the rest of his gang? He never went anywhere without them. She knew if she jumped out of the van and started running away from him, they'd appear from nowhere and help him get her back in the van. Alex paid for two tickets and they drove in. He picked a spot in the back, but off to the side. Being on the side of the drive-in would let them be by themselves. The other cars would be to one side of them. He backed the van into a spot and turned off the ignition. Getting up he went to the back of the van to fold down the bench seat.

As he started to fold down the seat Andrea said "You fold down that seat and I'll scream."

"Well she finally speaks. At least I got you to say something. All right I won't fold down the seat as long as you agree to come back here and sit to watch the movie. I'll turn the seat around and open up the back doors so we can see the movie. Is that alright with you?" he said rather sarcastically.

Andrea nodded her head. Alex didn't want a confrontation with her just yet. He knew getting close to her was going to be a struggle and he wanted to save his energy. After he got the seat situated he motioned for her to come back. Slowly Andrea moved to the back of the van. She sat as far to edge of the seat as possible, but Alex sat down right next to her. The movie started with previews of upcoming shows.

Just as Alex started to put his arm around Andrea, she said "I'm gonna go get some popcorn?"

"Oh no you don't" Alex said. "You're not going anywhere. If you want some popcorn, I'll go get some, but you're going to stay right here. You aren't to leave this van. This van is being watched and if you try to go anywhere I'll know immediately. Understand?"

She nodded yes. She knew she wouldn't get far if she tried to run so she just sat there. Alex got out of the van and started walking towards the concession stand.

Jason and Cindy were sitting quietly watching the previews when Jason decided he wanted some popcorn.

21

"Cindy I'm going to go get us some popcorn before the feature movie. Would you like anything?" he asked.

"Popcorn will be fine."

"Okay. I'll be right back then." He opened the car door and started towards the concession stand. As he turned back to wave at Cindy he noticed a blue metallic van parked off to the side of the drive-in. A couple of cars had blocked his view from seeing it before. He knew it was the same van he had seen earlier that morning and then leaving the Higgins place this afternoon. A tall muscular, rough looking guy was getting out of the van. He appeared to be heading towards Jason. Jason eyed him carefully. Who is this guy? Who's he here with? Continuing to watch him as he walked by he saw he was heading towards the concession also, so he followed directly behind him.

Alex noticed Jason watching him. What's this guy's problem? Alex wondered. I'm not bothering anyone. Why's he staring at me? Alex gave thought to confronting him and on any other night he would have tried to start to a fight, but not tonight. Tonight he wanted to focus all of his energies on Andrea. She was his prize for the night.

Jason continued following him inside. He wasn't doing anything unusual nor was he acting strange. Maybe this guy is all right after all, but his appearance kept telling Jason differently. Walking out they passed each other and Jason said "Hello."

Alex nodded his head and headed back to his van.

Jason went back to his car with the popcorn. He relaxed and started enjoying being with Cindy as the beginning of the movie started.

Andrea sat quietly in Alex's van. She didn't know what to expect from him but she wasn't about to let her guard down. Alex was sneaky and she knew it. She'd heard all he had to do was signal somehow and his gang would come running to his side. She kept trying to think of a way to leave, but she knew his gang was near and watching. She saw Alex heading towards the van.

"Brace yourself Andrea, here it comes" she said out loud.

Alex got into the van and handed her the popcorn and the drinks he had purchased. "Well, here we are, just you and me. All alone" he said putting his arm around her and pulling her closer.

"Really Alex, that's close enough," Andrea said.

"I don't think so," Alex said pulling her closer.

"Please Alex, don't. You're not going to get anything from me anyway!" she snapped. "So why bother trying."

"You think not, do you? Well, we'll see" he said letting go of her for a while as they sat watching the movie.

It might as well have been a blank screen for all she cared. She wasn't able to concentrate on the movie and wasn't really seeing any of it. Andrea knew it wouldn't be long before he would make his next move.

Alex sat thinking how delicious Andrea's full red lips would feel on his. He let his eyes wander father down her body. Slowly taking in every curve of her creamy white neck and shoulders, then to the swell of her breasts moving slightly with her nervous breathing. I want to hold her close and have the chance to see her womanly body. I can hardly wait. Soon I'll have you for my very own. You'll want me . . . there's no doubt in my mind he thought. Yet, he had an uneasy feeling about being with her. A strange feeling that he had been with her before. Something about her stirred some inner feelings. Feelings he couldn't figure out.

Andrea knew he was looking at her body as if she had nothing on. She knew all too well what that look of lust in his eyes meant. She had seen that look many times before in the eyes of other men.

He pulled her even closer and said, "Kiss me" as he placed his lips upon hers. Andrea tried to pull away. "Ah

. . . now, my kisses can't be that bad. Other girls enjoy them, so just let yourself go and enjoy them too."

"Please . . . may we watch the show. This movie is supposed to be good." Andrea said hoping he'd leave her alone long enough for her to figure a way to get out his van.

"May I have some pop now?" she asked, stalling for more time.

"Of course, Andrea darling, but only after I put a little something in it. It wouldn't do to have you drink only pop, now would it?" he said as he poured something into it.

She wasn't sure whether it was alcohol or a drug. Still, she sat there unprotesting. She knew it wouldn't do her any good anyway. Taking the drink from him she began to sip it very slowly knowing she would have to appear to be drinking it, or he would force it down her. She needed to keep her head about her tonight no matter what.

Andrea had no idea that Alex had put too much of a powdered drug in her drink for her to be able to handle even one little sip without feeling it's effects. They sat a while watching the movie. Alex was waiting for the drug to take effect before trying to make another move on Andrea. He knew once the drug took over she wouldn't be able to fight him off.

"Alex, I have to go to the little girls room. I'll be right back," she said. From the restroom maybe I can find a way out of the drive-in without him seeing me she thought. Knowing it was probably her only hope, she started to get out of the van. As she began to move her head started spinning so fast it made it very difficult to move.

"What did you put in my drink? My head feels as though it's going to spin right off," Andrea cried as she leaned back in the seat.

"Awh . . . my poor Andrea" Alex said. "Just relax and enjoy it. It won't be long and you'll be as high as a kite and enjoy doing anything. Anything I want you to do. You'll find it a pleasure to perform for me." Then he pulled her close to him again.

Keep fighting it she thought. Don't give in to the drug. If you do, he'll have you right where he wants you. It was hard to fight off his kisses, his hands and the effects of the drug all at the same time.

Alex was kissing her lips and then her neck. He was so adept with his fingers that he had undone a couple of buttons on her blouse before she realized what he was doing. I can't take any more from this man. I've to get out of here. But how? My head is spinning so fast. I can hardly move. I've never felt so weak.

"Alex, please stop . . . I'm getting sick. I think I'm going to throw up," Andrea cried.

He released her immediately and somehow she managed to jump out of the back of the van. She started running for the gate when all of a sudden his gang appeared. She had forgotten about his gang members. They certainly hadn't wasted any time in showing up. By the look in their eyes she knew they meant business. She began to panic as they started closing in on her. What am I going to do? Won't anyone help me, she thought. Probably not. Either they're involved in what they're doing and paying little attention to anything else, or they just didn't want to get involved. I don't blame them. What could anyone do against a gang and especially this gang?

Andrea turned around to see just how close they were. As she did, she stumbled and started to fall. She was about to hit the ground when some one caught her. Her heart leaped into her throat. Who has me? She was afraid to look, yet there was something very familiar about the touch. Forcing herself she looked up. It was Jason.

"Oh Jason, I'm so glad to see you! Please help me!" she said. Pointing at the gang of men standing just a little ways from them. "They're after me!" she continued as tears started streaming down her face.

Jason pulled her up and looking into her eyes he saw that she was crying. He hadn't seen her cry since she was very young. She never let anyone see her cry. He couldn't handle seeing her this way.

"Stay right here," he said pushing her behind him. Jason had noticed a commotion from over towards the metallic blue van and had gone to investigate it. As he neared the commotion he saw Andrea running with a group of guys running after her.

Jason confronted Alex "You'd better leave now."

"I don't think so. You have something I want and I'm not leaving without it" Alex stated.

"She's not going anywhere with you. Now leave!" Jason demanded.

"I said I'm not leaving without her!" Alex yelled.

"You'll have to get through me first!" Jason stated.

"Do you really think you can take all of us? There are four of us and only one of you." Alex said confidently.

Alex was sure Jason didn't have a chance against all of them.

"If you think you can take me . . . bring it on" Jason said stubbornly.

As Alex took a couple of steps towards Jason, his gang fell in behind him.

"Are you sure you want to take all of us on?" Alex asked Jason again.

"Like I said, go for it" Jason stated.

Jason knew it was going to take all he had to win this fight but he wasn't going to let them take Andrea.

Alex stepped back and let his gang close in on Jason. Then he headed for Andrea.

Jason made the first move by kicking Ed in the knee, forcing it to bend the wrong way. Then he hit Dick across his nose breaking it. Both of them fell to ground. Joe lunged at Jason with a knife. Jason jumped out of the way, but not before it hit his left forearm leaving a deep gash. Jason grabbed Joe's arm and managed to make him drop the knife. Finally, Jason managed to get Joe on the ground and after one final punch he knocked Joe out. Jason got up looking for Alex hoping he hadn't gotten away with Andrea. He saw Alex holding onto Andrea.

As Andrea fought to get away, Alex slapped her a couple of times cutting her lip. He was about to put her back into his van when he heard, "I wouldn't do that if I were you." Jason said standing firm.

Alex spun around to see Jason standing close to him and all of his gang rolling on the ground in pain or out cold. He pulled out a small silver revolver from underneath his coat. He still couldn't believe Jason had gotten through all of his gang.

"Now it's your turn. The other three were easy. Now, I'm going to give you the chance to walk away and not get hurt." Jason demanded. He had seen Alex pull the gun out. Jason was slowly moving towards Alex. He was within one step of him. He knew his reflexes were quick enough to deflect the gun before Alex could pull the trigger.

Without his gang to back him up and with as many witnesses' as there were around, Alex decided he needed to wait to take Jason out. He put his gun in his waistband and smiling at Jason said "Another time. Take this as a warning." Then Alex walked over to help his gang members up and they staggered toward their car and Alex's van.

Jason walked over to where Andrea was leaning on a speaker post. She was so weak she didn't think she could stand up on her own.

"Are you alright?" Jason asked her.

"I'll be fine," she said quietly, trying to get up. "Are you okay?" she asked looking up at him.

"I'll be better once I get you out of here" he said angrily.

He reached down to help her up as Cindy came running towards him.

"Oh Jason, I was so afraid something was going to happen to you." She hugged him and started kissing his face. Jason had some cuts and bruises but was going to be all right once he cleaned himself up and bandaged the cut on his forearm. All in all he had taken care of those guys rather easily. Cindy removed her scarf and was about to wrap his forearm with it, when he pushed her aside and turned back towards Andrea with a loathing look in his eyes.

Andrea had finally managed to stand up but was swaying a little. When she saw the look in Jason's eyes she stumbled backwards and fell down again. She knew that look meant he was very, very angry with her.

"Just what were you doing out with a piece of scum like that in the first place? I thought you were smarter than that! You told me you didn't have any plans for tonight. You lied to me!" He yelled at her.

Her head was still spinning, her mouth was bleeding, and now . . . now Jason was yelling at her like she was a child. It was just too much. She managed to stand up again. He's not going to treat me like a little girl and get away with it. I'm not about to tell him why I was out with Alex, nor why I can hardly stand up she thought steaming. He'd never understand in the first place. I'm not going to explain anything to him. Besides, he's not concerned about me anyway, he's looking at Cindy now who's all over him like a mother hen . . . and he's enjoying it. The scene made her sick.

Andrea yelled at him to make him look at her, "I find that is none of your business. I don't wish to talk about it. Please, if you and" (she looked angrily at Cindy) ". . .

28

Cindy don't mind, please take me home now," she said as she stumbled towards Jason's car.

Jason stood there staring at her. I should shake her and make her explain. But what I really want to do is make everything all right for her. To protect her and keep her safe and happy with me. Oh . . . but this still isn't the time to do so. He let his anger get the best of him.

"Very well. But before we go, fix your blouse. You look like you're advertising all of your wares, and here (he handed her his handkerchief) use this to stop your mouth from bleeding."

He wanted to take her in his arms and tell her he loved her. To tell her that he'd never let anything happen to her, but instead he grabbed her arm and pulled her along towards the car with Cindy still trying to hang all over him.

Andrea got in the car first. She thought about getting in the front seat so Cindy would have to sit in the back, but decided it wasn't such a good idea. Jason was angry enough with her. She didn't want to make him angrier. She got in the back and sat quietly.

"Well Andrea, I hope you realize that Jason just risked his life for you" Cindy said as she continued fussing over Jason. Andrea was getting madder by the moment. Cindy finally managed to use her scarf to wrap Jason's forearm to slow the bleeding.

Oh Jason, Andrea thought, how can you like such a whining woman. You could do so much better, but then again, you did choose her didn't you? You could have your pick of any woman in town but for some unknown reason you picked her. If he'd pick a woman like her, what makes me think he'd ever pick a woman like me? I wonder if Cindy is as sickening as I think she is, or am I just so jealous that she just seems that bad?

"Yes Cindy" Andrea finally said, "I realized that Jason risked his life for me. I am thankful and grateful, but that seems to be his job. He's always there when I need

29

him. Almost as if he just follows me around all the time" she added curtly.

You really don't understand do you Andrea, Jason thought. I'm not there because I'm supposed to protect you as part of my job I'm here because I love you. Oh damn it, will you ever understand? No. You may never know of my love for you unless you someday stumble upon it.

He was just as stubborn as she and he wasn't about to give her any hint as to how he really felt about her.

Jason said "Cindy, I didn't do anything for her that I wouldn't have done for you. In fact, I would have fought until death if it meant saving your life."

"Oh now I couldn't have that. That certainly wouldn't do me any good," she said as she placed a kiss on his cheek.

Andrea's heart felt like it had just been torn in two. He really did love Cindy. He just said he'd die for her. I guess all I can do is accept it and keep my feelings to myself no matter how bad it hurts.

As they got closer to her house, her mouth was really beginning to throb and her head was hurting.

"Jason" Andrea said "not a word to my folks about tonight and I mean it! They're not to know one single thing about what happened."

"We'll see" Jason said, "we'll see little one. Just how well you handle yourself when you get home will be half the battle. You know your parents always wait up for you when you're out. When you have to face them with that split lip, well, that won't be easy for you to explain. But I won't say anything unless I'm asked."

They pulled into the drive. Andrea jumped out of the car not even saying goodbye. She walked to the front door. From there she could see her parents setting in the parlor. She decided to go in the back way and just maybe she could get up to her room before her parents realized she was home. After all, it was only about eleven o'clock.

They never expected her home before midnight. Besides, Jason had a good point. How in the world was she going to explain this split lip?

Jason watched Andrea walk around to the back. She'll make it inside without them even knowing she's home. I should go take her in the front door and make her confront them, but I'll let her handle this one alone he thought. He and Cindy left to go to his place. He needed to clean up and take care of his arm.

Andrea slowly walked in the back door trying to be very quiet, only to run right into to Daniel in the kitchen. He was fixing himself a sandwich.

"What are you doing sneaking in the back way?" Daniel asked.

"Just felt like it" Andrea snapped while holding Jason's handkerchief to her mouth.

"Boy, you look terrible! What happened to you?" he asked.

"Nothing, I just feel ill" she snapped again. Her head was still spinning. "I'm going to bed."

"Just a second" Daniel said. "A guy by the name of Alex Longred was here looking for you today. I told him you were at the shop. Did he find you?"

"Yeah. I guess you could say he did," she said flatly.

"Hey, what happened to your lip?" Daniel asked.

"I bit it," she said. She knew he didn't believe her, but she also knew he wouldn't ask her about it again. "Night" she said. Then she crept up the back stairs to her room where she could feel safe again.

She headed to her bathroom to clean her mouth and take a shower. She scrubbed and scrubbed herself until she felt like she had no skin left. She hoped it would help her get rid of that dirty feeling she kept having. Looking in the mirror again, she hoped her mouth wouldn't show a bruise, just a little cut. Her head had finally stopped spinning, but she still had a really bad headache. Oh,

31

how I want to just forget everything that had happened to tonight. Putting on her nightgown she climbed into bed.

Shirley and Tom finished watching their late night movie and headed upstairs for bed.

"Is Andrea home yet?" Tom asked.

"I don't think so. At least she hasn't popped her head in to say good night. But then again, with the way she's been acting lately, it wouldn't surprise me if she didn't" Shirley said. "She had a date with some boy. He looked slightly familiar, but I couldn't place him. Maybe they're just having such a good time she's forgotten about the time. I really would like to see her enjoy herself. She's certainly seemed uptight lately" Shirley continued.

"I know what you mean," Tom said just as they heard screaming coming from Andrea's room. They went running. They found her tossing and turning in her sleep.

Andrea was screaming "No . . . no . . . Stop.... Stop it! Jason please help me!" Tom reached her bed first and shook her to wake her and then put his arms around her to stop her from twisting around.

"Andrea. Wake up! What's the matter? Please wake up baby. It's dad!" Tom said.

Andrea finally opened her eyes to see her father holding her.

"Oh dad, hold me tight please." Andrea begged as she put her arms around her father.

"Hey, is this my big girl scared by a bad dream?" Tom asked as he wrapped his arms tighter around her. She almost seemed like his baby again.

"Are you sure it was just a bad dream?" Shirley asked as she sat down on the bed beside them.

Andrea hesitated a minute. Should I tell them, she wondered? No. No, I can't.

"It was just a bad dream, just a bad dream," as she continued holding on tightly to her father.

"You sounded scared to death. You called out for Jason" Tom said.

"Well, you know he's always protecting me from God knows what" Andrea replied as she turned towards her mother.

Shirley looked at Andrea and noticed her lip bleeding. "What happened to your lip? It's bleeding."

What do I say, she wondered? Then she knew. "I must have bit it during the dream" she said feeling it with her hand. It had started bleeding quite a bit again and it hurt even more. She hoped her mother wouldn't look too closely.

"It can't be that bad. I'll go wash it off" she said as she started towards her bathroom.

Andrea stopped when her mother said, "By the way, you didn't say hello when you got home."

"I was so tired that I came directly to my room and went to bed," Andrea said hoping they'd believe her.

"Well, take care of your mouth and go back to bed. We're just around the corner if you need us. We'll talk more in the morning," Tom said as they were leaving her room.

"Andrea hasn't had any bad nightmares since, since she was very little." Tom said sounding very concerned.

"I know" Shirley replied. "I wonder what brought this one on?"

"I hope it's nothing," said Tom. "But we'll have to watch her closely to make sure she doesn't have anymore. We have to make sure that the past doesn't repeat itself."

Andrea lay back on her bed trying to calm herself down. In her dream, Alex had succeeded in getting his wish. That thought was more than she could bear. Heading into the bathroom again she took care of her mouth once more.

Lying in bed, she tried to sleep but sleep just wouldn't come, so she got up to look out her window. From her window, she could see Jason's cottage. Staring at it, she thought, Oh Jason, thank you so much for saving me tonight. What would I've done if you hadn't shown up? She continued staring at Jason's cottage. The lights were on inside so he was home. She thought about going over to talk to him just as the lights went out and Cindy and Jason came out the front door.

Stopping on the porch they stood staring at the stars. Jason placed his arms around Cindy as they kissed. Andrea had never seen him kiss anyone with so much passion. It was the kiss she longed to be hers. Jason, oh Jason, she thought as her eyes filled with tears till she couldn't see anything. It's just as well. She didn't want to see anymore. He loves Cindy. That was obvious. I'm just going to have to accept it. Walking over to her bed she buried her face in her pillow and cried herself to sleep. That was something she hadn't done in a long, long time. Not since . . . she was a very young child.

Chapter Two

Alex and his broken gang members returned to his place. They needed to take care of their wounds. Alex lived in a big old rambling house, a couple of hours away from Andrea's. His house was located far outside the city and way back off the road. No other houses could be seen. Alex lived with his guardian. His guardian never really cared about him. He just wanted Alex to stay out of his way.

Alex tried to sit down, but was so angry he couldn't sit still. Why did that guy irritate him so? Probably because he was the only man Alex had encountered that wasn't afraid to stand up to him and his gang. Alex was afraid that this guy was capable of beating him. That thought frustrated him very much.

This guy also appeared to be ready to protect Andrea with his life. But he still wanted Andrea. There was an unseeable force drawing him into Andrea's life. It wasn't just the fact that she was a beautiful woman. It was something else . . . but what was it? Why do I feel like this?

"What are you going to do about this guy?" Joe asked Alex.

"I don't know yet" Alex stated. "But I'm sure as hell going to think of something. Somebody find out who he is and what his connection is with Andrea! Also, find out who the girl was that was with him."

"Maybe we can get to his girl and use her as a trap. I just don't know if his girl will have the same effect on him that Andrea does. I don't know which one will cause him the most pain. Should we get his girl or should we get Andrea? Whatever we do, we'll have to use one of

35

them as bait to trap him. Then we'll be able to finish him off for good" Alex said frustrated.

"How about using both of them?" Ed asked.

"That's it! That's it! Now there's a situation that he'd never be able to resist. I bet he'd do anything to keep both of them safe" Alex exclaimed.

"Now Joe, get out there and find out all you can about this guy. Who he is, where he lives, what his connection to Andrea is, where he works, where he spends most of his time and report back to me as soon as possible," Alex demanded.

"Ed you go find out who the girl is. What her name is, where she lives, where she works, etc. and report back to me ASAP!" Alex demanded again as he slammed his fist down on the desk.

Ed and Joe headed out the door, leaving Alex and Dick to plot out what they would do with them once they got a hold of them.

Jason woke the next morning feeling quite sore and he moved very slowly while rising. I feel like I've been through a war he thought. Walking into the bathroom and looking at himself in the mirror he saw a couple of cuts and bruises on his face. After removing the bandage from his arm, he realized his arm looked pretty bad. He winced with pain as he placed a new bandage over the gash. How in the world will I to explain these cuts and bruises to the Higgins family? I haven't been in a fight for years. I hope they don't ask me too many questions he thought.

Jason finished washing, got dressed, and headed for the Higgins house. Joining them for breakfast two days in a row was rare and he probably shouldn't, but he wanted to see for himself that Andrea was going to be all right after last night. He knew he couldn't just walk in and ask about her. He was going to have to eat breakfast with them and act normal while hoping Andrea would show up so he would know she was okay. Entering the kitchen, everyone was at the breakfast table, except for Andrea.

"Good morning Jason" Shirley said, "glad you decided to join us again this morning." As she turned to see him she said "Oh my goodness whatever happened to you?"

"I got into a little scrape last night" Jason responded, as he slowly sat down.

"Marabel, please come over here and tend to Jason," Shirley said.

"No, never mind Marabel. Please, continue what you're doing. I've already cleaned and dressed my cuts," Jason stated as he gestured for her to continue what she was doing.

"How many did you get into a fight with?" Tom asked. "I've never known you to get so many bruises before." Tom noticed how carefully Jason was holding his arm and assumed it must be pretty bad. He also noticed the long-sleeved shirt Jason was wearing which was unusual for him to wear during warm weather.

"A handful," Jason said grinning, "and you should see the rest of them. They look worse than I do. Where's Andrea this morning?" He wasn't sure if he should ask about her or not but he just had to know if she was all right.

Daniel looked over at Jason. Jason and Andrea had something in common. They both looked terrible after last night. Just a coincidence, he doubted it.

"Last time I looked in on her, she was still sound asleep. I didn't want to wake her. She didn't sleep very well last night," Shirley said. "As we were going to bed, she started screaming in her sleep. She hasn't done that for a good many years. Oh, and she also called out to you for help. Do you have any idea what's been upsetting her so lately?"

Jason sat quietly for a minute then replied "No, can't say as I do. But I'd be happy to talk to her about it if

37

you'd like." He didn't enjoy lying to the Higgins family, but he didn't want to get Andrea angry with him either.

"That won't be necessary," Tom said. "I'm sure she'll tell us when she's ready to let us know what's up."

Jason was sure Tom had sensed that he knew more about Andrea's problems, then he was admitting. Still he didn't want to lose what trust Andrea had in him, so he said nothing more.

I sure hope she's all right. She looked pretty bad last night when I left her here. I should have looked in on her after I took Cindy home, he thought.

After finishing their breakfast they were walking into the parlor to plan the day's activities just as Andrea came walking down the stairs.

"Good morning" Andrea said pausing on the steps.

"Good morning" Shirley responded. "How are you feeling this morning?"

"Fine mom" she replied.

Andrea looked over at Daniel. Oh my God, I forgot all about running into Daniel when I got home, she thought. He saw my mouth and we talked about it. He knows I didn't bite it during my dream. Did he say anything? Did Jason give me away? She got very nervous.

"Really mom, I'm fine now. I'd like some toast for breakfast though," she said eyeing Jason carefully for any clue that he had told her parents all about last night. Apparently he hadn't, nor had Daniel. My parents would be extremely upset with me right now if either of them had said something.

"Marabel will fix you something I'm sure," Shirley said and with that Andrea continued on towards the kitchen.

Andrea's head still hadn't quite cleared, but she really did feel pretty good. She was still a little shook-up and her mouth was pretty sore. She was tired from lack of sleep, but she was going to be okay. Jason didn't look too good this morning though. I hope he's all right. He didn't seem to want to move his arm very much. I'm going to have to ask him when no one else was around just how bad his arm is she thought.

"Why Miss Andrea, you finally decided to get up?" Marabel asked.

"Please Marabel, no lectures this morning. I'm really not up to it" Andrea said sitting down to the breakfast table. Andrea realized years ago that Marabel always knew more of what was going on then anyone else in the house. It was no use hiding anything from her. She always found out anyway.

After a few minutes Marabel said, "Here Miss Andrea, drink this and I'll get your toast. It'll clear your head in no time." She handed Andrea a large glass that contained some potion she had concocted.

Andrea looked up at Marabel surprisingly and said "What do you mean it'll clear my head?" No one knows about my head she thought. I didn't tell a soul that Alex drugged me. How does Marabel know?

"Miss Andrea, it's all over town about last night. Or at least those of us who were at the bakery this morning know about it. Cindy was at the bakery telling anyone who would listen about what happened at the drive-in last night," Marabel said.

"Marvelous, just marvelous," sighed Andrea. "I was so hoping I could keep it from mom and dad. Now they'll find out for sure." She paused thinking a minute, "But how did you know about my head? I didn't tell anyone about that, especially Cindy."

"Word gets around about scum like Alex and his gang. He may live a ways away from here, but things get said. Drugging his dates is something he likes to do. I wasn't sure if he'd done that to you but I thought I had better be prepared just in case. You just confirmed that he did so I was right in having that drink ready for you" Marabel said.

"You were one of the lucky ones that was able to get out of his van. I've heard of what happens to the girls who don't. You really don't want to know what he does to them. But promise me this, that you'll never go out with him again!" Marabel begged.

"I promise. Thanks for the drink. I know it'll help. You always have the cure for everything" Andrea replied. Then she thought. I promised her I wouldn't go out with him again, but I'm still not sure how I'm going to be able to stop him. I can still hear his threats of hurting my family and me. I thank God I was able to get out of his van in time.

Shivers ran up and down her spine just thinking about what could have happened to her if she hadn't. Getting angry she decided it was time someone stood up to Alex and his gang, and I'm going to be the one to do it. Andrea thanked Marabel for the drink again and walked out of the kitchen.

Walking towards the parlor she could hear her brother George telling her parents about the ruckus at the drive-in last night. He mentioned Alex and Jason, but he said he didn't hear who the girl was. He said everyone in town is talking about it.

She heard her dad say, "Who was this girl you saved last night?"

At this point she rushed into the room, "Do you need help in the shop today, mom? I feel up to helping out today if you need it. I had fun working yesterday."

Andrea was rattling on about helping her mother in the hopes of changing the tide of their conversation.

"Andrea, please you're interrupting" Shirley said. "Yes I can use your help today if you're sure you're up to it. Now, Jason, you were about to tell us who the girl was that you saved from that beast."

"Saved . . . why from what?" Andrea asked looking at Jason and pleading with her eyes for him not to give her away. Please don't tell them it was me . . . please . . . she begged secretly.

George answered, "At the drive-in last night. Some guy named Alex and his gang went after some girl and Jason saved her from them. It's a wonder he isn't in worse shape than he is. After all, there was four of them and only one of him. Now who was the girl?" George asked again looking at Jason. Then he saw Jason looking directly at Andrea and knew all too well who the girl was.

Andrea kept pleading with her eyes.

Jason looked at Andrea and into those beautiful pleading eyes. How can I give her away? How can I tell them with her looking at me like that? He was helpless when he looked into those eyes. He knew he couldn't hurt her by telling them the truth.

Jason finally stated "I don't believe you know her, and I personally believe that she'd rather not have her name mentioned where Alex is concerned again. I'm certain she plans on staying away from him from now on. At least that's the way I believe she should feel. So I think it's best to leave her name out of this story."

Inside Andrea sighed a long, relieved sigh. Her eyes thanked Jason over and over again. In her heart she knew he wouldn't give her away.

Looking at Andrea, Jason saw relief written all over her face and he knew he had made her happy. He also noticed George watching at the two of them. He was sure George had figured everything out. Jason had missed Tom taking it all in too.

"George, did anyone say what they knew about this Alex guy and his gang? I haven't seen them around here before. I'm curious as to why they were here and what they wanted," Jason asked.

"The clerks in the bakery seemed to know all about this guy and his gang. They didn't seem surprised about what happened. I'll ask around today and see if I can get you some more information" George said.

Jason sat a while and then stated, "Well I'd better get busy. I have a lot of work to finish today and I need to keep the boss happy," he said looking over at Tom and nodding as he left.

Andrea watched Jason walk out of the room and then said, "I'd better go get dressed."

Looking at her mother she added, "I'll be ready to go with you in a few minutes."

"Are you sure you're up to it?" Shirley asked her.

"Of course mom" Andrea said as she left the room. She yelled back "I'll be just fine."

Tom looked over at Shirley sitting in her favorite chair sipping her morning tea. Shirley hadn't noticed the look Andrea had given Jason nor the exchange of nods between them, but he had. He was sure they knew a lot more about last night then they were admitting and he intended to find out what it was.

Andrea headed straight for Jason.

"Jason!" Andrea yelled as she caught up with him on the back porch. "Thank you for not telling my folks. I know it took a lot for you not to say anything, but you know they'd skin me alive if they ever found out." Andrea pulled her robe tighter around her, for it was a cool morning.

Jason could see every curve of her body now. Oh how I want to hold her body close to mine he thought.

"That's alright. But you know your name isn't going to be left out of the story for very long. I'm sure they'll find out soon enough. Then we'll both have to answer to them. But we'll have to cross that bridge when we come to it. Besides, I know George picked up on what was going on in there. If he could, so could your father. I'm not looking forward to the time when he figures out what we have covered up. Especially me," Jason said.

Andrea moved closer to Jason and looking into his steel blue eyes, she reached up and gave him a big hug and a kiss on his cheek. Leaning back with her arms still around him she stared deep into his eyes. I love you so much. Can't you see how much I need you? I want you to hold me in your arms? I want to place my lips on yours? Should I take the chance and kiss him right now? No. I can't . . . I can't. He has Cindy. He loves Cindy. I've got to let go of my feelings for him. But that's so hard to do. Her thoughts bothered her very much.

Jason was looking down into her eyes. I love the feeling of her arms around me and the feeling I get when she touches me. She looks even more beautiful in her robe. Her eyes are glistening like a fresh fallen snow. Placing his arms around her waist, he pulled her closer to him wincing in pain as he did. It hurt his arm to pull her close, but he didn't care. He wanted, no needed, to feel her body next to his. Their bodies seemed to mold together. She smelled so sweet. She was so soft and warm.

A fire had started in his loins and he wanted her now! I want to tell her I love her, and as he looked into her eyes he thought he saw . . . was it possible? Could it really be true? Did her eyes show love for him? Did he detect a desire for him? Before he could tell, her eyes started showing pain, a hurt that came from somewhere deep within her and she pulled herself away. He wanted to pull her back, but something inside him told him that once gain this wasn't the right time.

As Andrea pulled away she asked, "How bad is your arm?"

"It hurts but it'll be okay. I'll just have to take it easy on that arm for a couple of days" he said wondering why she pulled away from him with such a pained look in her eyes.

He wanted to ask her what she had been thinking but instead he said, "I'd like to know who's been talking about what happened last night. It sure traveled fast," he said.

"I know," she said. "Marabel told me as she was fixing my breakfast. She already knew too."

"Who?" he asked her.

43

"I don't believe I should tell you" Andrea said hesitantly.

"Who was it Andrea?" Jason demanded taking her by the shoulders and staring deep into her eyes.

"It . . . it was Cindy. She was telling everyone at the bakery this morning and . . . well, you know the rest," Andrea said looking down.

So it was Cindy, he thought. I should have figured. She never could keep her mouth shut. If you want the whole town to know something, just tell Cindy. She made it easy to get information about town because she blabbed it to everyone she came in contact with. It took her no time at all to let everyone know. Why do I keep hanging on to her anyway? What attracted me to her in the first place? I sure don't remember what it was.

Andrea was watching him. What's he thinking? She could tell his mind was racing fast. Does he believe me? Does he think I said it was Cindy so he'd get angry with her? She couldn't tell by looking into his eyes. His eyes were always so hard to read. They rarely revealed his emotions.

"I've got to get ready to go work with mom. See you later" Andrea said as she started walking away.

"You too" he said.

Sitting in her room, Andrea started thinking about Jason and Cindy. So now he knows Cindy is no angel. But he had to know that already. I just hope he doesn't hold it against me for being the one to tell him. Eyeing herself in the mirror, I am pretty, she thought. Much prettier than Cindy. Will Jason ever notice me as a woman and not as someone he has to protect, or as his little sister? Someday I hope he will, she thought, he's just got too. She dressed and headed towards the stairs.

"I'm ready" Andrea told her mother as she came down the stairs.

"Okay, let's go" Shirley said reaching for her coat. Shirley was still concerned about Andrea. She still looked exceptionally pale. I need to keep a close eye on her today, she thought. Knowing Andrea, she won't tell me if she isn't feeling well. I'll have to make that call myself.

Tom was in the study doing paperwork regarding the many functions of operating a cherry orchard. As he was going over some paper work he stopped to look out the window and he saw Jason. Tom knew Jason cared a lot more for Andrea than he cared, or dared, to admit. Tom was thankful he did, but was it possible for him to care too much for Andrea? He wasn't sure. He thought they loved each other, but they were always pulling each other in opposite directions and hurting the other one in the process. He knew one thing though . . . they both knew more about what happened last night then they had let on. The two of them were certainly hiding something this morning. But what was it? And why? Putting his work down he grabbed his jacket and walked out to where Jason was working.

"Jason" he said as he approached him, "this morning when we were discussing the ruckus at the drive-in, you acted liked you were covering up something. So did Andrea. Do you care to talk about it?"

Jason sighed and looked at the tools he was holding in his hands. What do I say now? He wondered.

"No, I don't wish to talk about it." God how I hate to mislead Tom, he thought.

"If it involves Andrea in anyway, I think I have a right to know" Tom added.

"Well yes, I suppose it does involve Andrea, in a way." Jason took a couple of seconds to compose his thoughts. "The girl involved happens to be a very close friend of Andrea's and she asked that her name be kept quiet so that it wouldn't get spread all over town," Jason stated.

"That's it?" Tom asked sounding surprised.

45

Jason hesitated, oh how I hate to continue to lie to him, "Yup, that's all."

Tom knew better. He knew Jason wasn't telling him the truth, but decided not to push it further. Jason always did the right thing in the past and this time he was sure it would be no different.

The Flower Shop was getting quite crowded when Sue came rushing in looking for Andrea.

"Andrea, are you all right? Oh my God, look at your mouth!" she said.

"Shhhh" Andrea whispered. "Follow me into the stock room."

Sue asked Andrea "Is what I heard about you true?"

"I'm afraid so" Andrea said as she stared at the floor. She felt so ashamed for letting such a thing happen.

"Is your mouth all right?" Sue asked.

"My mouth is going to be fine. It's just a little sore. It's nothing really," Andrea said as she placed her hand on the side of her mouth.

"What about Jason?" Sue asked.

"He's okay. He has a few cuts and bruises, but he'll be fine." Andrea answered.

"It sure was a good thing he showed up when he did" Sue remarked.

"Yeah, I don't know what I'd have done if he hadn't. I shudder to think of what might have happened to me" Andrea stated softly.

"Andrea" Shirley yelled "I could sure use some help out here. I have customers lining up."

"I'm coming" Andrea replied. "I'll have to talk with you later," she said to Sue as she returned to help her mother. Sue followed her out, said goodbye, and left.

Chapter Three

As usual Alex rose late on Saturday. He was still trying to devise a solid plan to trap Jason. He knew it had to involve Jason's girl friend or Andrea, and if possible, both. Alex and his gang had spent most of the night trying to think of something, but all of their plans had holes in them. Containing Jason was definitely going to be a problem. They had to get to Jason where he was most vulnerable.

Alex sat quietly thinking. Ed had done his research well returning with the name of Jason's girlfriend. Ed also found out that Jason is an employee of the Higgins family. That he is one of their orchard managers and in charge of the grounds' crew of 'Cherry Wood Mansion.' He also discovered that one of Jason's duties is to watch over Andrea. This made it obvious to Alex that he felt obligated to protect Andrea at all costs. His livelihood depended on it. This gave Alex an idea. Calling his gang together they made their plans. This time Jason would have no way out.

Andrea and her mother were rushing around the Flower Shop attempting to keep up with the mid-day rush of tourists as Mrs. Taylor, one the town's most elite ladies, entered.

"How are you today, Mrs. Taylor?" Shirley asked.

"Just fine. Is my order ready for tonight's party? I wanted to personally pick it up. I want to be sure everything is exactly right," Mrs. Taylor said.

"Yes your order is ready. I put it up myself earlier this week" Shirley said smiling at Mrs. Taylor.

"I certainly hope to see you and your family tonight," Mrs. Taylor added.

"Andrea, please go in the back and get Mrs. Taylor's order" Shirley said to Andrea.

Oh my goodness, she thought, I've forgotten all about the Taylor's Cherry Festival Ball being tonight. We really need to attend. Almost everyone in town . . . who's anybody . . . will be there. Our family has to be represented.

As Andrea walked out of the back room with Mrs. Taylor's order Shirley said "There, just as you ordered. The best silk flowers' money can buy."

Then Andrea carried Mrs. Taylor's order out to where her driver waited.

"Please put them on my account" Mrs. Taylor said as she watched Andrea carrying the order out the door. As always Mrs. Higgins does such an excellent job, she thought, it must be nice to have such a creative talent.

"We'll see you this evening," she said as she was leaving.

"Andrea" Shirley said as she pulled her aside, "please run home quickly and tell your father that we must attend the Taylor's Cherry Festival Ball this evening. Apologize to him about such a late notice. I completely forgot all about it. Also tell Daniel and George. Tell them I would like them to attend too. I know it's probably too late for them to get dates, but I'm positive there will be more than enough unescorted ladies to keep them company. And, speaking of unescorted ladies, see if Jason is available to escort you."

"Okay mom, I'm on my way" Andrea said heading out the door. Arriving at home she found her father still working in his study.

"Hi dad" she said entering the study. "Got some news for you. Mom forgot all about the Taylor's Cherry Festival Ball tonight. She wants all of us to attend. Would you tell Daniel and George about it when you see them? Mom wants them to attend also. Have you seen Jason lately? I need to talk to him."

She's talking very fast, Tom thought. Andrea only talks fast when she is nervous or upset. I wonder what's the matter?

"He was working by the central barn the last time I saw him. I'll tell Daniel and George when they get back from the orchards. I doubt they'll be any happier about attending tonight then I am. I suppose we must keep up appearances though. I'm sure most of the town will be there," Tom said.

"Now, dad . . . it's the kickoff of the Cherry Festival. Get into the spirit. This time of year always means lots of parties and once you get to them you always have fun" Andrea said. "I'll see you later. I have to find Jason."

"Just a minute" Tom said. "Jason told me the girl who was involved in the incident at the drive-in last night was . . . (he paused as he saw her face go pale white) a good friend of yours. She's going to be all right isn't she?" he asked.

"She's going to be just fine once she gets over being so shook up" she said nervously.

"Why in the world would she go out with a hoodlum like him?" he asked watching Andrea carefully. She seemed even more nervous.

"It's quite a long story dad. Let's just say she didn't have much of a choice" she said, hoping she was hiding her lies well enough.

"How about your date last night?" Tom asked. "Did you have a good time? Where'd you go?"

"Really, dad . . . my date was kind of boring and we were at the drive-in too; although I had no idea so much was going on till it was all over." I hate lying to my father, she thought. Besides, he usually knows when I'm lying to him. I hope he doesn't find out this time. He's always trusted me and I don't want to lose his trust.

"I'd better go find Jason," she said. Walking out the room she added "See you later."

Turning back to his work Tom thought she's lying. Just as she and Jason had done this morning. What are they covering up? Was she the girl involved last night? No, it couldn't possibly have been her. Daniel told him that her lip was bleeding when got home last night so she hadn't bit it while dreaming. She had lied about that too. They were hiding something this morning, and I want to know what it is! They haven't heard the last from me regarding this matter he thought.

Walking out on the porch Andrea stood watching Jason as he worked. How do I ask him if he can escort me to be the ball tonight knowing that he probably already has plans with Cindy, she wondered? Would he really rather be with Cindy than be with me? She continued staring at him. He looked so masculine. His brown hair blowing gently in the wind. He already had a bronzed tan from working outside in the weather. As he used his muscles to turn the tools he was using you could see each ripple in his arms. It must hurt him to use his arm like that she thought. Then she let her eyes wander over his entire body. What a magnificent physique he had. Just looking at him made her face flush. Oh well, just go other there get it over with. Just go out there and ask him she told herself as she started walking towards him.

"Hi" Jason said as he saw her approaching. He'd seen her standing on the porch watching him. He would have given anything to know what she had been thinking as she stood on the porch he thought.

"Hello" she said looking strangely at him.

"Do you need something?" he asked.

"Umm . . . it's just that . . . mom forgot about the Cherry Festival Ball being held at the Taylor's tonight, and she thought . . . well . . . I . . . she hoped you'd . . . be available to escort me. That is, if you're free. If not, Daniel would probably be available to escort me, but not without a lot of complaining. And you know how adamant dad is about me having an escort," she added nervously.

"Of course I will" Jason said without hestitation. "I'll call Cindy and let her know that our plans for tonight are off." Then he added, "She'll understand. After all, it is part of my job."

Why did I add that, he wondered? That's definitely not how I feel. His statement had made him sound so cold and distant.

"Thanks a lot. I was hoping you'd be able to" Andrea stated coldly. After all, it's his job. He sure knows how to hurt me she thought. Without saying goodbye, she turned and headed towards the house staring at the ground as she went.

Watching her go, he knew he had upset her, but something inside him stopped him short of telling her he was sorry. That isn't how I feel about escorting her. Why did I say that? He couldn't come up with an answer.

Walking into her bedroom she finally let her tears fall. She didn't want anyone to see her cry. She lay down on her bed again and just let herself have a good cry. It seemed she had been doing a lot of this lately. Finally getting control of her emotions she picked up the phone and called her mother. "Mom, if you don't mind, I'd like to stay home and start getting ready for tonight" she said hoping her mother would agree.

"It's quieted down considerably since you left, so I think I'll close up early. Stay home and please ask Daniel to pick me up in about hour" Shirley said as they hung up.

As Andrea hung up, she thought I'm gonna get through to Jason. I'll make myself look so irresistible and beautiful tonight he'll forget all about the fact that escorting me is part of his job! I want him to be proud he's out with me.

51

As Daniel entered his father's study he said "Dad, I'm on my way to pick up mom. But I thought I should tell you, Alex, the guy who was involved in the incident at the drive-in last night was here yesterday looking for Andrea. He said he went to college with her and that she had invited him to stop by if he was ever in town. Do you think it was Andrea with Alex at the drive-in?" Daniel remembered how upset she had been when she got home. He knew she was going to be very upset with him for telling this to their father.

"I'm pretty sure of it, but not one word about this to your mother. This would really upset her," Tom said.

"Okay dad. I'm off" he said as he left.

Tom figured it had been Andrea. That must have been what Andrea and Jason were trying to cover up. But why would she go out with a guy like Alex? She said the girl had no other choice. What did she mean by that? He'd have to do a little investigating on his own. Of course he'd have to talk with Andrea about going out with this Alex guy. "That's something that's never going to happen again," he said out loud.

After finishing his work for the day Jason went to call Cindy. Picking up the phone he dialed her number.

"Hello" Jason said as Cindy answered.

"Hi" Cindy said. "I was hoping it would be you. So what are we going to do tonight?"

"Well that's way I called. I have some bad news for you. I'm sorry but we won't be able to go out tonight. Mrs. Higgins forgot about the Taylor's Cherry Festival Ball and they have requested me to escort Andrea. Sorry for the late notice but I only found out a little while ago myself," Jason said hoping she would understand and not raise a fuss.

"Oh Jason. I was so looking forward to tonight since our date last night was ruined. I hoped we could make up for it tonight if you know what I mean. You spend an awful lot of time with Andrea. Sometimes I think she owns you. I think she means a lot more to you than I do" Cindy whined.

"Now Cindy" Jason said in a tone that normally made her shut up.

"She's just a pretty little rich kid who thinks every time she snaps her fingers, people should jump and come running and you know . . . that's exactly what you do!" she yelled.

"Listen Cindy" he said "that's enough. I should have known better then to think that you'd understand. Or that you'd even try to understand. I won't have you talking about Andrea that way. And another thing, what's the big idea of telling everyone about last night? You knew Andrea didn't want anyone to know. Of course, you had to run your mouth, as usual. Now it's spread all over town. Sometimes Cindy you have one hell of a big mouth!"

"You don't have to swear at me" Cindy snapped.

"Well think about it. If you would just use your head, it would keep you out of trouble" he said. "Going out with Andrea will be a relief after going out with you. After all, she doesn't hang all over me like you do."

"If that's the way you feel, maybe you should just spend all of your time with that little hussy!" Cindy yelled.

"I will. After all, you let me down by telling everyone about what happened last night. This is it Cindy we're through Cindy. Goodbye!" Jason yelled as he slammed the phone down.

Cindy slammed her phone down too. Oooh, that man makes me so mad she fumed. He's always been wrapped around Andrea's little finger and he probably always will be. I hope she makes him miserable. He'll come to his senses and come crawling back to me and when he does, boy, will I make him crawl! Cindy hoped she was right.

Paula K. Kohl

It's done Jason thought. We're through. This wasn't the way I wanted to end it, but she left me no choice he fumed, then he headed to the bathroom to clean up.

Chapter Four

The Cherry Festival Ball is always a formal affair. Hosting the event is rotated amongst the areas' most elite families. This event marks the beginning of the National Cherry Festival activities held throughout the area for the next eight days. This annual festival is a celebration of the cherry crops grown in this part of the country. Millions of tourists from all over the world come to this festival and each year its' attendance grows. The festival begins with the ball and culminates with the Cherry Royale Parade. The Higgins family has hosted the ball many times and their cherry orchard is always represented in the Cherry Royale Parade.

Everyone was ready for the ball except for Andrea. They were waiting in the parlor for her and had been waiting for a while. They needed to leave soon for the ball.

Shirley wore a light blue dress with a floor length flowing skirt. The dress had a square cut neckline with a sheer blue lace overlay on the bodice making her look like royalty.

Tom, Daniel, George and Jason were dressed in their black tuxedos. They looked quite handsome but Jason stood out amongst them. His tuxedo had been tailored to fit his body perfectly. His broad muscular shoulders and his bronzed face made him look even more handsome.

Walking out of the parlor and into the entryway, Shirley called up to Andrea. "Andrea we're ready to go. Hurry up dear, or we're going to be late." To be a little late was fashionable, Shirley thought, but she didn't want to be too late.

"I'm coming," Andrea answered. "Just one more minute."

The rest of the family walked to the entryway hoping Andrea meant what she said and that she would be coming down any minute.

Andrea took one long last look at herself. I sure hope Jason notices this dress. I've certainly worked hard enough to get it to look just right, she thought. Straightening her dress and adjusting a curl on her forehead she said to herself 'here goes nothing' and she headed towards the stairs.

Marabel was standing behind her and added, "You'll be the bell of the ball." Marabel had helped Andrea for over an hour to get the look she wanted. She knew Andrea was doing this for Jason even though she hadn't said a word. She didn't have too.

As Andrea started down the stairs, her father stopped and stared at his daughter. Her brothers, who never gave a thought to paying their sister a compliment, were amazed at how elegant she looked.

Jason stood in awe as she descended. Andrea had never looked so beautiful to him. She was wearing a light yellow silk dress cut low to show the fullness of her breasts and styled to show off her lovely white shoulders. The dress was fitted to accentuate her small waist and flowed into a graceful full skirt. Her hair was in ringlets with soft flowing curls about her face. She was strikingly beautiful. Jason wanted to run to her, put his arms around her and kiss her full red lips that were glistening slightly. If only she knew how desperately I want her. I want to be her lover and companion. His face grew warm as he watched her continue to float gracefully down the stairs.

Tom stepped forward, "My, my" he said proudly. "My little darling has turned into a beautiful woman. I'm going to have to keep a watchful eye on you this evening, or should I leave that up to Jason?" he said as he winked at her.

"Andrea, you do look lovely," Shirley said "and now we really must be leaving."

Jason's heart beat faster as she moved closer to him. He reached for her wrap and gently placed it on her shoulders. As his hands touched her shoulders, he felt a fire start in his loins. He smelled her soft sweet perfume and was barely able to control his emotions.

Andrea stood still as Jason's hands lingered on her shoulders. A warming sensation begun where his hands were touching her. She knew this feeling. She always got it when he touched her. She'd seen the look in his eyes as she came down the stairs and knew she had made quite an impression on him.

Tom helped Shirley with her wrap and they walked to their car and left. Andrea and Jason got into Jason's car and headed towards the Taylor's home. Daniel and George drove off in Daniel's car.

As they were pulling out of the drive, Jason finally managed to say to Andrea "You look absolutely beautiful tonight" and he smiled lovingly at her.

"Thank you" she said, and a few seconds later. Then added "I hope you didn't have any big plans for tonight with Cindy. I mean, I hope your escorting me isn't too much of an imposition."

"No, of course it's not" Jason said. Why does she always have to bring up Cindy? "I'm always happy to escort you anywhere," he added.

"Yes, I know. It's part of your job. You made that perfectly clear earlier" she stated coolly. "You certainly weren't too happy about escorting me home last night. As a matter of fact, I believe you were sorry you got involved with saving me from Alex and for my interfering with you and Cindy" she stated as she stressed Cindy's name.

"That's not true and you know it. Yes I was upset with you, because you had gone out with this Alex guy in the first place. But I wasn't upset about your interfering with Cindy and me. Besides . . ." Jason stopped talking.

"Besides what?" she asked looking over towards him trying to sense just what is was that he was feeling.

"Nothing . . . just forget I said anything," Jason said looking a little upset. She knew that look and knew when he didn't want to tell you something, there was absolutely no use in pleading with him.

"Why did you go out with him anyway?" he finally asked her. After a few moments of silence he added "I know you know him from college. He stopped by the house yesterday and Daniel talked with him. I passed him as he was leaving. He's obviously trouble. So why were out with him?" he asked again.

What do I say? Should I tell him? Then she got angry. Who does he think he is! I don't have to tell him anything she thought.

"I don't think that's any of your business," she added angrily.

"It most certainly is my business since I had to save you from this guy. Why Andrea?" he asked again.

"It's none of your business so stop asking me!" she yelled.

Jason decided to drop the subject. He was obviously upsetting her and that was the last thing he wanted to do tonight. He wanted them to have a nice enjoyable evening together. If he continued to question her, it would only start their night out badly and that would surely make it end badly as well.

They pulled into the Taylor's driveway right behind Shirley and Tom. The valet was there to park their cars. They waited for their turn. It appeared as most of the guests had already arrived. The outside of the house was decorated majestically. White twinkling lights were everywhere. As the valet opened the doors to their cars they could faintly hear music coming from the ballroom.

Shirley, Tom, Daniel and George entered the Taylor's home followed by Jason and Andrea.

The inside of the house was decorated just as magnificently as the outside. The same white twinkling lights, flowers, ice sculptures, draped ribbons and of course, cherry blossoms and cherries. The arrangements Mrs. Higgins had made seemed to fit in perfectly with theme Mrs. Taylor used for decorating. The doors to the veranda were left open allowing a cool summer's evening breeze to flow through the ballroom. Andrea was delighted at the sight. She forgot all of her troubles and began to enjoy to the evening.

As guests entered the ballroom, they were formally announced. This ritual had started in the early 1900's by the Taylor's ancestors and is still practiced faithfully today at their parties.

"Announcing Mr. and Mrs. Thomas Higgins of the Lake View Cherry Orchard and sons Daniel and George" the butler stated as they where entering the ballroom. The sounds of music and laughter filled the air. Everyone was having a wonderful time. Mr. and Mrs. Taylor came forward to greet Tom and Shirley.

Next to be announced were Andrea and Jason. Entering the ballroom archway, Andrea placed her hand on Jason's arm holding it gently.

The butler continued, "Announcing Miss Andrea Higgins and her escort Mr. Jason Steele of the Lake View Cherry Orchard." As he did so, everyone in the ballroom turned to stare at the handsome couple. A murmur spread through the guests as they turned to see the striking couple as they made their way into the ballroom. Men seemed to be mesmerized with Andrea's graceful appearance and the ladies were swooning over Jason.

As they stepped down from the entryway, the gala started again as the guests greeted them.

"I do believe we made quite an impression this evening" Andrea said when they were finally able to head towards their reserved table.

"Of course we did. I'm out with the most beautiful woman in the whole world," Jason said as he squeezed her hand and looked into her beautiful eyes. "Andrea I meant exactly what I said. You truly are the most beautiful woman in the world."

But Andrea didn't hear a word he said as the music started up just as Jason began talking. Andrea smiled at him and nodded her head. He knew she hadn't heard him.

Jason couldn't keep his eyes off Andrea's since they arrived. Her radiant smile seemed to glow. It made him feel warm inside seeing her so happy and full of life. She smiled at everyone who acknowledged them. Of course everyone knew she was there, she made sure everyone noticed by her grand entrance into the room. But then again, she always had that affect on people wherever she went.

As they were standing near their table, Mr. Taylor came over. Mr. Taylor made sure he was the one to greet Andrea as he had other motives going through his mind.

"Andrea, you look so lovely this evening; but of course, you always look lovely my dear" Mr. Taylor stated bending to kiss her hand. As he did so he moved closer to her, dropping her hand slowly and allowing his hand to brush lightly over her breast.

Jason saw this incident, but decided to be still. Andrea would let him know when she had had enough. She always did.

"Jason, nice to see you here this evening. By the way" Mr. Taylor continued "where is that young woman of yours? I believe her name is Cindy?" he said moving closer to Andrea and brushing her body with his.

"I don't know where she is. I'm here with Andrea this evening" he stated and with that, Jason reached for Andrea's hand saying "Shall we dance?" for Andrea had given him that look of 'please help me.'

"Yes, I'd like that very much" she said sighing with relief.

"Thank you for rescuing me from that leech. I'm sure he was going to keep trying to get closer to me and then pretend his innocence about touching me" Andrea said placing one hand in Jason's and the other on his shoulder. They started to waltz across the room. Mr. Taylor walked away from their table in disgust.

"You're quite welcome," Jason said. Jason was holding her close as they began to dance.

Andrea could feel warm sensations throughout her entire body and her heart began beating faster. She couldn't help but wonder what it would be like to be held in his arms in a fit of passion. To kiss him and join their bodies as one. Ahh, but that was just wishful thinking. Cindy was his lover. She had seen them last night. She had seen that kiss. The kiss he had given so willingly to Cindy. The kiss she longed to be hers.

"Jason, did something happen between you and Cindy today? You seem to be very touchy every time her name is mentioned" she asked looking into his eyes.

Jason was quiet. Then looking deeply in her eyes he wondered why she always brought up Cindy. Is she truly concerned? Just what does she want to hear me say? Does she want to hear we're through or that things all right between us? Jason was bewildered.

"We had a little disagreement this afternoon," he finally said.

"It wasn't about having to be here tonight with me was it?" she asked almost apologetically.

"No" Jason said, "but that's all I plan on saying about the subject. I don't wish to discuss her anymore tonight."

Just then Tom came up. "May I?" he asked gesturing to dance with his daughter.

"Why of course dad" Andrea said as Jason politely placed her hand in Tom's and returned to their table.

61

"You seem to be deep in thought. Is something wrong?" Tom asked as they circled the room.

"Not really dad. It's just that I'm confused. There are times when I think I have Jason all figured out and then he goes and does something to mess me up again," she said.

"Well don't let it bother you too much. He tells me the same thing about you" he said smiling at her.

Andrea looked over towards Jason. Two young ladies had already joined him, and were flirting with him. Before this evening is over, I'm going to be a very jealous person indeed she told herself.

"Speaking of you and Jason" he continued "I think you two are keeping something from your mother and I regarding last night's incident. Do you feel like talking about it anymore?"

"Dad, I already told you all I knew this morning. The girl who was involved is a good friend of mine and doesn't want anyone knowing it was her" she said.

"Andrea you're lying" Tom stated sternly. "I happen to have heard that the girl involved was you. Is that true? Were you the one?"

Andrea gasped and missed a dance step. She was no longer able to lie to her father.

"Yes dad. It was," she said dropping her head.

"Why didn't you tell me the truth in the first place?" he asked.

"I couldn't. I was too ashamed," she said staring at the floor.

"Why did you go out with him?" Tom asked, knowing it had taken a lot of courage on her part to admit it.

"I told you I had no other choice" she stated bluntly. "Does mom know?"

"No, and I intend on keeping it that way if possible," Tom said as the song ended.

Before Tom could ask any more questions or escort her back to her table, Andrea was inundated with gentlemen requesting the privilege of dancing with her. It's customary to let young ladies dance with their escorts and fathers before asking for a dance. With each new song she had a new partner.

She tried keeping an eye on Jason, but it was difficult. Jason was also in demand by every lady present. Jason was dancing with a new partner almost often as she was.

Andrea despised having to make small talk with each of her dance partners. Many of them thought women were stupid and the topics of their conversations were quite boring. She was getting tired of dancing. She was secretly hoping the orchestra would take a break so she could rest.

Andrea noticed that Sheryl Taylor, their hostess's daughter was paying a lot of attention to Jason. Andrea felt the jealously in her flare up as she watched Sheryl carefully massaging his sore arm, and gently kissing the faint bruises on his face. I wonder if she knows he received those injuries because of me, she thought. Jason appeared to be soaking up every bit of the attention and sympathy she offered. Sheryl kept moving closer and closer to him. Watching this really irritated her.

Jason wanted to be with Andrea tonight . . . all night . . . and have her all to himself, but that was not to be. It seemed that every party they attended together always turned out this way. There were always so many admirers around her he never got time to be just with her. Just once couldn't it be different? She always looked like she was truly enjoying herself. I don't think she cares what I'm doing. I can't take much more of watching her smiling sweetly at her dance partners and moving so gracefully across the dance floor with someone else. I'm going to have to do something to take my mind off her he thought.

"Sheryl would you like me to get you something to drink?" Jason asked.

63

"Don't you think it's getting a little warm in here? Why don't we take a walk on the veranda instead?" Sheryl said smiling. Not waiting for his answer she grabbed his good arm and led him out on the veranda. Then she steered Jason to a secluded spot where she stopped and fanned herself. Then pretending to faint she fell towards Jason so he would have to catch her. Jason quickly reached for her and gently pulled her up. As he pulled her up she wrapped her arms around him.

Andrea noticed the direction in which the pair had headed and got very upset. How dare he leave with her! I want him to be with me! Am I that easy to forget she wondered?

It always winds up this way. He spends most of his time with other women and I spend my time with other men. It's no wonder he doesn't mind escorting me, she thought. He doesn't have to spend much time with me and gets to spend his time with many different women. Escorting me is only part of his job, she reminded herself. He had said so himself this afternoon, but, oh how she had hoped tonight would have been different. She wanted to make him forget that being with her was just part of his job. I want to go home. I want to forget this night ever happened. Her thoughts were giving her a headache.

Andrea was dancing with Ted Jones. He's a respectable young man, she thought. Suddenly she knew how she was going to get to go home. She stumbled while dancing with him and put her hand up to her forehead.

"Andrea, what's the matter?" he asked holding her tightly and helping her to her table.

"I've just got an awful headache. I think I need to sit down," she said still holding her hand on her forehead.

"Let me get you something cool to drink," he said as he helped her sit down. "Will you be all right?"

"Yes I think so," she said.

Ted quickly returned with a drink.

"Thank you," Andrea said taking a drink and leaning back in her chair.

"I think I should go home. Would you be so kind as to find my parents?" she asked quietly.

"Certainly, I'll find your parents, but why bother them when I can take you home myself? That is, if you'll let me? It would be a pleasure," he added.

"Thank you Ted, that's very nice of you," Andrea stated.

"I'll go get your parents," he said as he left looking for Shirley and Tom. He quickly found them and related what had happened.

Shirley immediately came over to Andrea.

"I knew you weren't feeling up to par. I should have suggested you stay home. Will you be all right? Do you want me to come home with you?" Shirley asked feeling her daughter's forehead.

"No, mom, really, I just need to go home and lie down," she said quickly removing her mother's hand. "I'll be fine. There's no need for you leave the party."

"I'll go look for Jason and tell him you wish to go home now. He shouldn't have strayed so far away from you," Shirley said. She was irritated with Jason for having left Andrea alone. After all, he was her escort and it was exactly this type of thing an escort should be responsible for. She'd see to it that in the future he stayed closer to her side no matter who wanted to dance with her or him.

"No, mom," Andrea said. "Ted said he'd gladly take me home, so please, don't bother Jason . . . just tell him when you see him that I've left."

Tom walked up behind Shirley and noticed the hurt look in Andrea's eyes as she spoke of Jason. Damn, he said to himself, why don't those two stop playing games with each other. She loves him and he loves her, but neither of them wants to admit it. One of these days I'm going to sit them down and point it out to them myself. I can't sit back and continue to watch them hurt each other much longer.

"We'll see you at home," Tom said. "We'll look in on you when we get there. We won't be too late." He had a feeling she wasn't ill at all.

Jason was still out of the ballroom with Sheryl as Andrea and Ted prepared to leave. Taking one last look around the room and not seeing Jason, she left hanging on to Ted's arm. She knew it wouldn't be long before the older ladies would begin gossiping about her arriving with Jason and leaving with Ted. Obviously they had nothing better to do. She was right. They had hardly left when their tongues started wagging.

Well Jason, Andrea thought, I hope you're happy. I'm leaving so you won't have to bother with me anymore. I gave it my best shot and lost. I lost him to Sheryl or Cindy or whomever. It's obvious he doesn't want me. I'm not going to get in his way anymore. She got into Ted's car and they headed towards her home.

"Are you feeling better now?" Ted asked her. "Has the fresh air helped you any?"

"Yes, Ted, I believe I'm feeling better. I appreciate you taking me home. I didn't want my parents to have to leave on my account, but this type of party gets a little boring at times," she said.

"Yah, I know what you mean" Ted said. "I was glad to have a reason to leave. Especially with you." Ted reached over and tried pulling Andrea closer to him. Andrea ignored his passes. The ride to her house was a short one so she felt safe in ignoring him.

Andrea leaned back in her seat and closed her eyes. She was thinking about Jason, and didn't realize that Ted had turned towards Miller Hill instead of heading towards her house.

Ted turned off the main road and on to a two-track road leading to a secluded area at the top of the hill. As he did so, Andrea opened her eyes and realized he wasn't taking her home.

"Ted where are we going? You're supposed to be taking me home!" Andrea demanded.

He parked his car, turned towards Andrea and put his arms around her.

"Andrea I've longed to hold you my arms" he said trying to kiss her.

"Ted! Just what do you think you're doing?" Andrea demanded trying to pull herself away from him.

"I heard all about you last night. I figured if you went out with a guy like Alex, you'd certainly go out with me and make it a very interesting evening," he said as he continued pulling her closer.

Andrea managed to pull herself away from him "And just what did you hear about me?"

"I told you. I heard that you went out with Alex Longred, a guy who's the leader of a gang. One can only assume, that a guy like that dates girls for one reason and I'm sure he chooses those 'types' of women to date. After going out with a guy like that, I figured you might prefer a more refined type tonight," Ted said smugly.

"I didn't do anything with him, and I'm not about to do anything with you either" she said trying to slap his face. He quickly grabbed her arm, stopping her hand before it reached his face. As he pulled her closer she reached over him, took his keys out of the ignition and threw them out the window into the bushes.

"Hey, what did you do that for!" he yelled. At that same instance, she slugged him in the groin area, pushed open her door and started running, slipping on the under brush. Her high-heeled shoes were definitely not appropriate for running, much less in this type of setting. She turned around to see if Ted was following her. He wasn't. He must be searching the bushes for his keys, she thought. That would be a sight. Ted in his tuxedo, crawling around the bushes. Maybe that'll teach him not to assume she was such an easy mark for him, or anybody else for that matter. Pulling her wrap tighter around her shoulders she started down the two-track road towards home. Andrea didn't know that a much greater danger lay waiting for her.

Chapter Five

As closing time approached, Alex and his gang members sat watching the Soda Fountain where Cindy worked. Cindy's boss had just left and she was preparing to lock up for the evening. Since Jason had cancelled their date for the night, she had decided to work. She was still so upset about her break-up with Jason she didn't see Alex approaching.

"Hello there" he said pushing his way past her.

Cindy jumped back. "What are you doing? What do you want?"

"Look . . . just do as I say and you won't get hurt" he stated.

"What?" Cindy asked. She recognized him from the drive-in. What did he want? Was he going to rob the place? It was hard to believe this was happening. "What do you want?" she asked again.

"I want you. You're going to be my hostage," he said signaling to his gang.

"Okay guys, take the money out of the cash register. And you," he said pulling out a gun and pointing it at Cindy, "just act normal and I promise nothing will happen to you. At least not yet," he added.

"Why do you want me?" she asked in a frightened voice.

"Just open the cash register," Joe demanded.

Cindy opened the cash register and Joe took the money.

"Now come with me," Alex said as he pushed Cindy out the door and towards his van.

Why does he want me as a hostage? My parents don't have enough money to hold me for ransom. Just what is going on here? She wondered.

Alex pushed Cindy into the back of his van. His gang climbed in beside her.

"Hey Alex," Ed said from the back where he was sitting next to Cindy, "let's just keep this one," he said as he eyed her breasts. "She looks like a healthy one."

The look in Ed's eyes made Cindy very afraid. What did they want her for.

"Listen you guys . . . leave her alone," Alex said. "We've got to figure out how to get the news to Jason that we have her and what we'll do to her if he doesn't come to us peaceful like. Now put this blindfold on her. We don't want her to know where we're going."

So that was it, Cindy thought. Alex wants revenge. He wants Jason and he's using me as bait to get him. How clever, she thought. One problem though. Jason and I are through. We're no longer an 'item.' Now that we're no longer together, I don't know whether he'll come after me or not. Her mind raced. What am I going to do? One thing's for sure I always manage to make the most out of every situation, I can this time, too.

They drove for what seemed like hours to Cindy before the van stopped. Cindy didn't know where they were but she assumed it had to be Alex's home.

"Take her in the back way and up to the attic. Don't let her make any noise as you go. I don't know if my uncle Lance has left for his business trip yet. If he's still here I don't want him to know she's here," Alex said as they led her in the back entrance.

The attic was musty smelling and dusty, but you could see where the spider webs had been brushed away. A bed had been set up. Also a little table with a bowl and pitcher of water on it were setup beside the bed.

"Tie her hands together and tie the rope to the bed post. Leave her a little bit of walking room. Later we'll just lock the attic and keep the key," Alex said.

Looking straight into Cindy's eyes Alex added, "You can scream all you want. No one could possibly hear you, so if I were you, I wouldn't waste the energy. Lance never comes near this part of the house. I guess you could say this is my very own private wing. Besides, Lance may not even be here."

He was laughing as he turned to his gang and asked "Now how do we get the message to Jason letting him know we have her?"

Cindy watched Ed tie her hands together and then tie the rope to one of the bedposts. Looking around the room, it was obvious to her there was only one way out of the attic and she knew she'd never get past Alex's gang.

"First things first, Alex" Ed said. "You have your fling with her then it's our turn! We can let Jason know we have her later!"

Alex slowly walked towards Cindy. He grabbed her and pulled her towards him. He placed his lips on hers, and with his tongue he forced her lips apart. She felt as though she was going to throw up. She managed to pull herself from him.

"Please don't" Cindy cried. "Please don't. I'll do anything you want me to, but please . . ." Before she could say anymore he tried to kiss her again.

"Come on honey, you might find that you like my kisses more than Jason's. You'll find out that I do it better," he said as he attempted to kiss her again. Cindy bit his tongue.

"Why you little bitch" . . . and with that, he slapped her so hard across the face she fell backwards onto the floor and went out cold.

"Put her on the bed and lock the door behind you. No one touches her before I tame her, understand?" Alex stated as he stalked out of the room. His gang waited patiently for Cindy to regain consciousness. As soon as she did, there was no waiting for Alex. They decided they would try her out for themselves.

Joe moved slowly onto the bed as the others watched. Just as Joe was reaching for her Alex came walking back into the room.

"Get the hell away from her," he demanded. They all scrambled away from the bed. "I thought I told you no one was to touch her until I had finished with her!"

"We . . . we were just getting her ready for you," Ed answered.

"Like hell!" Alex said.

"Well, she's ready and waiting for you now. Go ahead. Take her. We'll wait our turns," Joe interjected.

Alex stood there looking at Cindy lying on the bed. She did look appealing. He let his eyes wander slowly down her body. He did want her. He went over to her and bent down to kiss her.

"Please, Alex" Cindy begged. "Don't do this to me."

He kissed her forcefully as he pressed his body down against hers.

"Please . . . please." Cindy continued begging, "I'll do anything you want me to, but please don't do this to me! I'll help you trap Jason," she cried. "I'll do anything to help you trap him, but please . . . please stop!" The thought of him raping her made her ill. "I'll help you figure out some way to get him. I know how he thinks, so I can help you, but please don't touch me," she pleaded.

Sitting back Alex thought, that's not a bad idea. With her on my side, it should make it easier to trap Jason. She knows all his weaknesses, his habits . . . this could be easier than I thought. With her helping me, things should go smoother. He got off the bed.

"Untie her," he said. "And you," he said looking at Cindy "get control of yourself."

Cindy sighed with relief. At least for the time being they would leave her alone. Saving herself meant she was going to have to help Alex trap Jason. She wasn't going to enjoy trapping Jason, but her life was on the line.

What of it anyway, she thought, I don't mean anything to Jason now anyway.

Cindy sat talking with Alex in an attempt to come up with a foolproof plan to trap Jason. Finally they came up with the plan of Cindy going to the ball and asking to speak with Andrea. She would say that she desperately needed to talk to her in regards Jason. She was to say that it was so important that it couldn't wait. Cindy was positive that Andrea would feel obligated to see what was so important. Andrea never could resist anything that had to do with Jason. She would easily fall into their trap. Ed, Dick and Joe would to go to the Higgins house and leave them a message stating that something awful would happen to Andrea if the Higgins family went to the police or caused them any trouble.

Alex and Cindy got into Alex's van and headed to the ball. Cindy felt it was best if she asked for Andrea and then led her out to Alex's van. At that point it would be easy for Alex to get Andrea into his van and take her back to his place. All Alex needed to do was drive and Cindy would handle Andrea.

Alex was beginning to take a liking to Cindy. It seems that she thinks along the same lines as I do. She appears to understand me, and why I need to do away with Jason.

Cindy was helping Alex for a couple of reasons. First and foremost was to keep Alex's gang from raping her and, secondly she wanted to get revenge on Jason for dumping her. If Andrea got hurt in the process, it would make it all the sweeter.

Ed, Dick and Joe left to go to the Higgins house. Figuring they had plenty of time to get to the Higgins house and get out before they would be returning or before Alex and Cindy would get back, they decided to take the back roads to the Higgins residence.

As they were driving down the back roads, they saw a figure walking on the side of the road in front of them.

"Someone is pretty stupid to be out walking alone so late at night," Joe said. "Hey it's a woman. Anyone for a little fun?"

"God, look! "It's Andrea!" Ed blurted out.

"It sure as hell is!" Dick said. "Let's nab her and get back to the house. Alex is never going to believe this. As soon as we get her to the house somebody needs to go tell Alex that we have her."

Andrea saw car lights coming and hoped it was someone she knew who would be able to give her a lift. She was getting cold, her feet hurt, and it was still a long walk home. As the car pulled closer, she looked into it and realized just who it was.

"Oh God, no" she said. "Please not them." She took off running again, but she stepped in a rut, her ankle twisted and she fell. She tried to get up, but she couldn't. Dick grabbed her arm.

"You aren't going anywhere but with us," he said.

"Please let me go" Andrea pleaded trying to pull her arm away.

"Ain't no way" Dick replied. "Alex would kill us if he ever found out we had you and let you slip through our fingers. Come on, let's go."

She was hitting him trying to make him let go of her. He pulled her up anyway and dragged her back to the car. Dick threw her into the car with the rest of the gang who made sure she couldn't get out as they headed back to Alex's place.

Jason and Sheryl were busy on the veranda. Jason politely kept fending off Sheryl's advances.

"I think we should go back inside now," Jason said. "We've been out here for quite a while. I'm afraid we'll be missed if we don't go in."

Sheryl and Jason walked back into the ballroom. Sheryl had strategically placed her hand on his arm so that it looked like he was hers. Sheryl's face was flushed making it obvious to everyone what had taken place on the veranda. Oddly enough though, Jason looked completely composed, as if nothing had happened. The ballroom was still full of people and the music continued. Jason scanned the room for Andrea. He couldn't see her anywhere.

One of the butlers came forward and announced he had a message for Miss Andrea Higgins. Jason walked over towards the door and after listening to part of the butler's conversation stepped into the entryway.

"Just what do you want with Andrea?" Jason asked staring straight into Cindy's eyes.

"I must speak with Andrea," Cindy said trying to avoid looking at him.

"And I just asked you why?" Jason demanded taking a step towards her.

"It's important that I speak with Andrea and Andrea only," Cindy stated. She was beginning to get quite nervous.

"All right" Jason said and he asked the butler to please have Andrea present herself at the front entrance.

"But I intend on standing right here and listening to every word you say to her," he said as he turned back to Cindy.

Cindy's mind was racing. I hadn't planned on this. How in the world am I going to get Andrea outside and away from him? What I'm doing is going to be harmful to Andrea. Jason suspects something's up so he isn't going to just let her leave with me.

"Mr. Steele," the butler said, "I've just been informed that Miss Andrea Higgins has already left the celebration. She left about 45 minutes ago. Mr. Ted Jones took her home."

Just then Tom came walking into the entryway. "What seems to be the problem?" he asked as he spied Cindy standing at the door. He figured it was just a lover's quarrel, but if he could help Jason out of an embarrassing situation, he would.

"Andrea left?" Jason asked Tom.

"Yes, she left about . . . oh . . . 45 minutes ago with Ted Jones. She wasn't feeling well so Ted volunteered to take her home. Why?" Tom replied.

"Why didn't she tell me? I would have taken her home," Jason answered.

"She said she didn't want to bother you. After all, you appeared to be rather busy," Tom added nodding towards Sheryl who had come to stand a little ways from Jason. She was blushing brightly.

"Damn" Jason said under his breath. She knew I was outside with Sheryl after all.

Cindy was listening to what they were saying. Since Andrea has already left I won't have to make up something to say to her with Jason standing right here listening. This puts a new a twist in our plan. Alex and I are going to have to come up with another way to get to Andrea, she thought.

"Well in that case, I'll just be on my way. I'll catch her later. Thanks," Cindy said as she started backing away from the door.

"Just one minute," Jason said as he grabbed her arm. She managed to pull it loose as Jason continued, "What did you want with Andrea anyway?"

Cindy turned and started running. Jason looked past her to see whom she was with. He could hardly believe his eyes. Cindy was heading straight towards Alex's van, and Alex was in the driver's seat. Why?

Cindy turned around and looked back towards Jason. She saw a look of hatred come over his face as she continued running.

Alex saw Jason following Cindy, so he started up the van and opened the door for her. They pulled out of the driveway just as Jason was about to grab the door handle.

"What the hell went wrong?" Alex asked Cindy as they both sighed with relief.

"Andrea had already left. When the butler announced he had a message for her, Jason came to the door instead. I didn't know what I was going to do," Cindy stated, gasping for air.

"I don't know what to do now," Alex said disgustingly. "Let's go back to my place and try to devise another plan."

Jason ran to his car and sped over to the Higgins house. He wanted to see if Andrea was there and if she was all right. He also was afraid that Cindy and Alex were on their way there. He knew Cindy had heard Tom say that Andrea had gone home ill. Jason hadn't forgotten Alex's warning and he was positive he still wanted to get to Andrea. Jason parked his car and ran into the house.

"Andrea are you here? Andrea are you home? Andrea are you here?" he yelled as he ran upstairs to her room. Her bedroom door was open but there was no sign of her, or any indication that she had been there since earlier in the evening.

Alex and Cindy arrived at Alex's and went inside.

"It was a good try Cindy, but with Andrea gone, "Alex shrugged his shoulders, "Well, we hadn't figured on that happening." They continued up the stairs.

"You know you're my kind of girl. You think like me and I think you feel like me," he said and then placed his arms around her and pulled her close. He began kissing her, and surprisingly Cindy returned his kiss.

I'm becoming attracted to him, Cindy thought. I do kind of think like him. We both want revenge on Jason. If I can't have Jason then no one can, she thought.

Opening the attic door, they were both shocked to see Andrea sitting in a chair gagged and tied up.

"How the hell did you get her here?" Alex asked as he rushed into the room.

"It was real easy," Ed said.

"How?" Alex asked again as he walked over closer to her.

Andrea eyed him very carefully.

"She was wandering down the road we was driving on, all by herself and all gussied up like she is. She put up a fight, but not enough for me," Ed added.

Ed stood staring at Dick. It was Dick who had gotten Andrea and put her in the car. He was the one that Alex should be rewarding, but Dick kept quiet. Ed could take care of Dick with no trouble at all, and Dick knew it only too well. No, he wouldn't make any trouble for Ed.

"So, Andrea . . . welcome to my humble abode. I certainly hope that the guys have made you comfortable. I know the accommodations here are not exactly what you are used to, but it's the best I can offer you since you require being locked up," Alex said eyeing her carefully.

"I'm gonna remove this gag from your mouth. Don't get any big ideas about screaming, 'cause there ain't no one around to hear you anyway," he said as he untied the gag.

"Just what do you want with me anyway?" Andrea demanded staring straight into his eyes.

"Ain't we getting pretty demanding?" Alex scoffed. "You'll find out all too soon. Just get down off your throne for a while. You'll know what we want with you when I'm ready to let you know."

Turning towards Ed, Alex asked, "Where's Joe?"

"I sent him after you. He should be back soon once he sees you're not there," Ed said.

"When he gets back, we'll have to prepare our defense strategy so that we're prepared for when Jason shows up looking for her," Alex said, nodding his head at Andrea. They left the attic and waited for Joe to return.

Jason drove back to the ball, jumped out of his car and ran inside. He looked around to see if Andrea had returned. When he didn't find her, he went looking for Tom.

"Tom, I just came from your house and Andrea isn't there. Who'd you say she left with?" Jason asked gasping for air.

"Now calm down" Tom said, placing a hand on Jason's shoulder. "She left with Ted Jones. Really, such concern over Andrea being with Ted. Is it really necessary?" he asked.

"I think there may be some trouble," Jason said, still trying to catch his breath.

"Trouble? What kind of trouble?" Tom asked. "Or are you just jealous because she might be having a good time with someone else?"

"No, really, I believe there may be some trouble and one way or another I'm going to find out!" Jason responded.

"Does Cindy have something do with this? Why was Cindy looking for Andrea?" Tom asked stepping back a little from Jason looking concerned.

"I don't think there's enough time for me to go into all that just now. Let's just say that what happened last night at the drive-in, well Andrea was the girl I saved from this Alex guy. He was with Cindy tonight when she was here looking for Andrea" Jason stated.

"Oh, my God," Tom said. "Jason, I knew it was Andrea that you saved last night. If this Alex guy ever does anything to her again, I'll kill him! I'll get Shirley and head home. We'll meet you there. You can fill us in on what you know and then we'll decide what we need to do."

"I'm going to stop at Ted's house to see if he and Andrea are there" Jason hollered over his shoulder as he left.

Tom quickly found Shirley.

79

"We need to leave," Tom said gently urging Shirley towards the door.

"Is something wrong?" Shirley asked. The look on his face was worrying her.

"I'm not really sure, but right now there's nothing to worry about. Jason's checking it out. We need to find Daniel and George. They need to come home too. Jason may need their help," he added.

Jason drove his car straight to Ted's house. Pulling in the drive, he saw a tow truck unhooking Ted's car.

"Ted, where's Andrea?" he asked as he got out of his car.

"Who knows where she is. I really don't care!" Ted sneered.

"You were supposed to take her home. I've been there and she isn't! Now, where the hell is she?" Jason demanded as he slammed his fist down on the top of Ted's car.

"Cool it, Jason. If you'd have stayed with her at the party, this never would have happened anyway," Ted curtly.

Jason grabbed Ted by the throat, "Tell me where she is or you're sure as hell going to regret it!"

Ted knew Jason meant it. Ted was no match for Jason.

"Okay, okay, let go of me and I'll start from the beginning. When we left the Taylor's, I took her for a little drive out to Miller Hill and parked the car. We had a disagreement. She threw my keys in the bushes. That's why I had to have a tow truck bring my car in. I wasn't able to find my keys in all the weeds and brush. She jumped out of the car and started walking for home I assume. That was the last I saw of her. Honest," Ted explained.

Jason finally let go of him. "You mean to tell me you just let her start walking . . . a woman, all alone at night, on a country road? Ted, after I find her I'm coming back here to settle with you," Jason stated and then he left.

Jason turned his car towards Miller Hill hoping to find her. It was a long walk home. There was no way she could have made it back to her house yet. He drove all over the area and didn't find her so he turned towards Cindy's house. He hoped he'd be able to find a clue there as to just what was going on. He could feel that Andrea was in real danger. Why was Cindy with Alex? Did Alex force Cindy to do what she had done? Or did she do it out of spite? If he was forcing her, then why did she go running back to him? It was becoming more and more apparent to him that Cindy, in some way, was willingly helping Alex.

Jason pulled into the driveway of Cindy's house and hurriedly walked up to the door.

As he knocked on the door, Cindy's father answered it.

"Jason, come on it" Peter Crouse said motioning for Jason to enter. "What can I do for you?"

"Is Cindy here by any chance?" Jason inquired.

"No, we thought she was probably out with you. She never came home from work this evening," he said.

"I was afraid of that," Jason said as he sat down looking rather concerned.

"Is something wrong?" Peter asked.

"I'm not really sure," Jason said. "You see, Cindy and I . . . split up this afternoon. Then this evening, I attended the Taylor's Cherry Festival Ball as Andrea's escort. Then Andrea left and Cindy appeared at the ball looking for her. I saw that Cindy was with this Alex guy and they drove off. I think Alex was forcing Cindy to help him, but it sure didn't look that way. Then I went looking for Andrea and she's nowhere to be found" Jason gasped for air after having quickly related the events of the evening.

81

"You mean Cindy was with Alex? The guy who was at the drive-in last night?" Peter asked.

"I'm afraid so," Jason said shaking his head.

"I'm calling the police," Peter stated.

"No, not yet. We don't know if any crime has been committed or just what in the world is going on," Jason said. "I'll find her and make sure she's all right too. I have to find Andrea. I'm pretty sure that when I find Andrea, I'll find Cindy too. Just wait here and I'll get back with you."

Jason got back in his car and drove to the Higgins house. He quickly walked into the parlor.

"Has she come home yet?" he asked looking directly at Tom.

"No. We haven't seen her. What did you find out at Ted's?" Tom asked.

"Ted didn't head directly here. He took her to Miller Hill. There he tried . . . well I don't know what he tried but Andrea got very angry with him and threw his car keys in the bushes. She jumped out of the car and started walking home. Ted just let her go. I drove all around the area to see if I could find her. I didn't. Then I went to Cindy's house to see if Cindy could tell me just what is going on. She wasn't there. Her father said she didn't come home after work."

Jason sat down putting his head in his hands. Where is she? "I'm positive this has something to do with Alex and Cindy too. I just can't figure out what" Jason sighed.

"George, earlier I asked you to check into Alex. Were you able to get any information on him?" Jason asked hoping to get some answers.

"Yeah I did. It's pretty interesting and scary at the same time. Alex's last name is Longred. He's been attending the same college as Andrea. So they probably did meet there. He's been in and out of trouble with the campus police for years. Every time they arrest him for something, his uncle gets the charges against him

82

dropped. Apparently he doesn't have much family. He lives with his uncle Lance who just happens to be an attorney. Another interesting fact is that he lives about two hours from here in a secluded old house just south of Reed City." George paused as he heard his mother gasp and turn pale white. Tom immediately went over to Shirley.

George didn't understand why his mother was reacting so strangely to what he was saying.

Jason jumped up and said, "I'm on my way to Reed City. I've got to get to Alex and find out what he knows." He headed towards the door.

"Jason!" Tom yelled as the tried to catch up with Jason. "There's something I need to tell you. Do you remember . . ." but it was too late, Jason was already driving away.

George and Daniel looked at their dad and then at their mother.

"What's going on? What were you going to ask Jason if he remembered? Why are you two acting so strange?" Daniel asked.

Shirley looked at Tom. Her eyes were filled with fear.

"Now Shirley" Tom said. "We don't know anything for certain yet. Let's wait and see what Jason finds out."

"Mom, dad what's the matter?" George asked.

"Just wait. I'm sure it's going to be all right," Tom said. "Daniel, go ask Marabel to bring us something to drink. It's going to be a long night."

Daniel headed towards the kitchen.

Jason drove to Reed City. After hearing what George had found out about Alex, and the fact that his last name is Longred, Jason knew exactly where Alex lived. He drove straight to his place without a problem. His driveway was long and winding. The old house looked extremely eerie in the moonlight.

Jason parked his car and got out. He took off the jacket to his tuxedo and threw it in his car. If there was going to be trouble, he wanted to be able to move freely. He ran up to the door and beat on it. When there was no answer, he kicked it open and went inside. Alex was just coming down the stairs.

"You sure like to kick things don't you? What's your problem this time?" he asked Jason as they glared at each other.

"All right Alex, where are they?" Jason demanded.

"Where is who?" Alex asked sneering back at Jason.

"Do you mean me?" Cindy asked as she quietly entered the room.

"Yes, for one. Are you all right?" Jason inquired while looking at her, but never really taking his eyes off Alex. He didn't want him to be able to get the jump on him.

"Alright? Why, I'm fine. Your concern overwhelms me," Cindy said. "Why would you think differently?" she asked.

"Come on Cindy, just last night you were scared to death of this character" Jason said nodding towards Alex.

"That was before I got to know him," Cindy said putting her arms around him hoping to get even with Jason even if it meant getting more deeply involved with Alex.

"Where's Andrea?" Jason demanded turning towards the two of them.

"Andrea? Andrea who?" Alex asked slyly.

"I said, where's Andrea?" Jason asked as he walked closer towards them.

"Why I do believe you mean Miss Andrea Higgins" Alex said. "You're very protective of her aren't you?"

"Alex, if you don't tell me where she is, I'm gonna tear this place apart looking for her," Jason demanded.

"You've already ruined my door. But by all means, search the entire house, but you won't find her here. As a matter of fact, at this very moment I don't know where she is," Alex stated.

"Let me give you a guided tour. Alex has been so sweet to me, he's shown me his whole house" Cindy said taking Jason's hand and leading him up the stairs.

Entering the first room Jason said "Cindy, look, I know I hurt you badly, but I never thought you'd stoop so low as to do this to get even with me."

"You over rate yourself Jason. But I must admit that at first when Alex came along, he scared me to death. But not now. He's treated me well, and he saved me from being raped by his gang," Cindy said quietly. "I owe him something for that." She was smiling inside watching Jason squirm while they searched the house.

"You know I can tell when you're lying, Cindy. Now you tell me the truth. Where the hell is she?" Jason demanded.

"I don't know," Cindy stated.

Jason grabbed Cindy at the shoulders, shook her and stared straight into her eyes and asked, "Where is she? Tell me or I'll force it out of you. Don't force me to hurt you!"

Cindy stood staring back into those cold blue eyes and she could see something in them that made her blood run cold.

"Jason . . . I . . . we . . . she was here, but Alex had her moved. I think to a cottage his uncle owns. But he wouldn't let me hear where it is. I overheard him say something to Ed about it. Please don't tell him I told you, he'd kill me for sure. I can trust him just only so far. Telling you this, well, that would definitely do me in," Cindy cried hanging onto Jason as a tear slipped down her cheek.

"Do you have any idea where it might be?" he asked.

"I think I heard him say Hogsback Lake, but I'm not sure. I wasn't supposed to be able to hear what they said. When they started talking about where they were taking her, they talked even quieter. Hogsback Lake isn't too far from here, so it's a good possibility. His gang has had just enough time to get her there," Cindy said as she stopped crying.

"Thank you Cindy," Jason said. "Now you're coming with me!"

"No. I think if I give him a chance, he may turn out to be all right," Cindy said. "Besides, if you take me, he'll have another reason to want you dead. Besides he won't let me walk out of here. He'll fight you to keep me here. His honor would be at stake. His gang would have that much more of a head start on you too. You'd better go without me. There's no telling what his gang may have already done to her. They sure didn't waste any time with me."

"Are you sure?" Jason asked.

Cindy nodded.

"All right then," Jason said as he went down the stairs and walked straight past Alex giving him a glaring look.

Cindy came slowly down the stairs as a smile quickly spread across her face.

"Did it work?" Alex asked looking up at Cindy.

"Of course it did," Cindy said. "He took the bait, hook, line and sinker. See, I told you I could be very useful to you" she added smiling to herself.

"You certainly can," Alex said as he pulled her closer to him. "You certainly can," and kissed her.

Meanwhile, upstairs in the attic Andrea was fighting for her life. Alex's gang had plans for Andrea that, even Alex wasn't aware of. Cindy and Alex headed up the stairs. As Alex entered the attic, Ed and Dick were on top of Andrea. One had pulled her skirt all the way up and the other was attempting to unzip her dress.

Alex raged "Stop that! She's not to be toyed with. At least not yet! We'll have our fun with her when Jason is here. He has to be here to watch everything that we do to her . . . slowly and deliciously," he said as he eyed her lustfully.

"Now, we have to move her out of this house. Once Jason figures out that Cindy lied to him about where Andrea is, he'll be back. All we have to do is hide her. I've got it! We'll hide her in an old clothes bag and put her in the trunk of the car. When Jason comes back to find her, Joe, take her to my uncle's cottage. Let's get started. It won't take him very long to figure things out," Alex stated.

"Cindy" Andrea blurted out, "Why are you helping this scum of the earth? You know he's no good. Why don't you go to Jason and warn him?"

"Sweet Andrea . . . spoiled rotten Andrea! Jason called it quits between the two of us this afternoon, as I'm sure you're aware. After all, you're the cause," Cindy snapped.

Smiling to herself she said, "I'm sorry Cindy. I had no idea." If I get out of this mess, I'm going to work harder on getting Jason all for myself she thought. Their break up must be why he was so touchy tonight every time Cindy's name came up.

"Sure you are. You manipulate him every chance you get," Cindy sneered.

"I do not," Andrea snapped. "I had no idea he was planning on splitting up with you."

"Why you little liar! You knew it all along," Cindy snapped again.

"I certainly did not!" Andrea said. "I've done everything I could possibly do so you and Jason would stay together. Even though I've always thought he could do much better," Andrea stated.

"Why you little . . ." Cindy yelled as she swung her hand back and slapped Andrea's face.

Alex was standing a little ways away enjoying the fight between the two of them, but when Cindy slapped Andrea, that was enough. Alex grabbed Cindy's hand just as she was about to slap her again.

"That's quite enough Cindy," Alex stated.

Joe entered the attic with the clothes bag.

"I've changed my mind. I think we'll just keep her up here for a while longer. If we try to move her too soon, Jason will surely get suspicious. When Jason tries to rescue her, it'll be much easier for us to handle him on our own turf then out in the streets. He proved that last night," Alex said.

They left the attic leaving Andrea all alone. Now that Cindy had sent Jason on his wild goose chase, they had a little time to come up with a plan to trap him.

Once we have him what'll we do to him? Kill him? Torture him? No, we can't kill him right away. That's far too good for him. We'll put on a show for him with Andrea as the main attraction. Then slowly kill her. Next Cindy can have her turn to have fun with Jason and do with him as she pleases, Alex thought. Once Cindy is finished with him, then we can kill him. Alex's eyes appeared as if they were set afire as he became excited about the upcoming fight.

Chapter Six

Andrea sat up in the attic. Alex hadn't tied her up again so she was able to move about. I've got to find a way out of here she thought. She tried the door knowing it would be locked. She looked around for a window. She found a small window at the far end of the room. Looking out it she saw that it was four stories down to the ground and there was nothing outside next to the window for her to hang on to or use to climb down on. She wasn't going to be able to get out that way.

Jason would be coming back soon to look for her, but that was what Alex wanted. Who knows what Alex has planned? Maybe Jason won't come back. He was so mad at me for getting involved with Alex in the first place, maybe he feels I'm getting what I deserve. Maybe he doesn't care about me anymore. After all, he made an attempt to find me. Maybe he thinks his job is finished. If I'm never found, he won't have to bother with me again. "Oh that's nonsense," Andrea said to herself.

Andrea started walking about the room again. I've just got to find a way to get out of here she thought. Looking around, she spied an old trunk under a pile of boxes. She felt drawn to the trunk, so she moved the boxes and looked at the trunk. It looked like it was singed or had been burned as if it had been in a fire. Hmm . . . she thought, I wonder what happened to this. Continuing to look at the trunk, she kept having a strange feeling. It was like . . . like she had been here before. But that was impossible. Wasn't it? As she sat there, flashes of a man and a woman's face kept appearing in her mind and she thought she could hear someone yelling. Then Alex entered the room and she snapped out of it.

Walking over to her he grabbed her chin. "Well, my pretty little Andrea, don't look so troubled, nothing's going to happen to you. Not yet anyway. You might as well give up looking for a way out of here, it's absolutely impossible. Any hopes you have of getting away are foolish. As for your precious Jason coming to save you, as you know he was here once but he left. Cindy sent him a wild goose chase looking for you. He'll figure it out soon enough though. Then he'll be back, but he'll never make it up here. This time he won't be so lucky as to get past my gang. Then we'll bring him in here alive, just barely alive. Just enough to comprehend what we have planned for you." He lit his cigarette and stared at the flame on the match. Andrea noticed a strange look come over his face as he stared at the match. As she was watching him, she saw reflections of a little boy holding a match. Shaking her head she looked at Alex again. His eyes seemed to be aflame. He shook the flame out then smiling at her he left.

Andrea was confused. Why do I keep having these strange feelings in this room? She began to shiver from being outside in the night air and her feet still hurt from walking so far. Her ankle was swelling and hurting quite badly. Wrapping herself in a blanket from the bed, she began to get warm and heat helped ease the pain in her ankle. She began to relax and fell asleep. She slept for over an hour then woke with quite a start.

She had been dreaming about a fire. Standing up, she looked over at the trunk again. Something was compelling her to open it, telling her to look inside. Slowly she opened the trunk. Inside were some old clothes. There was a woman's dress, a man's suit and some pictures. They were of the same people she had seen flash in her mind a while ago. Underneath the dress was a little baby doll. Andrea pulled the doll out and carefully placed it in her arms. It looked old and fragile. She had to be careful not to break it. The doll also looked

90

like it had been in a fire. Suddenly, it all came back to her. She sat back on her knees and started rocking the baby doll and started to cry. All of sudden the floor of the room felt very hot under her feet. She cried even harder.

Jason went straight to the police station instead of heading towards Hogsback Lake. Cindy had given him a grand performance, but his instincts told him that she was lying. She'd given him the information all too freely. He knew Andrea had to be in that house. He also knew he was going to need all the help he could get in order to get her out of there safely.

Explaining the situation to the police, it became apparent to Jason that they were going to be absolutely no help to him, whatsoever. The police explained that unless he was able to provide evidence that Andrea had, in fact, been forced to go against her will, there was nothing they could do. They agreed with him that Alex was very capable of taking her against her will, but there was no evidence of a kidnapping. Andrea hadn't been missing long enough. Jason would just have to wait. They agreed to patrol the area and keep an eye on the house, but they said that was all they could do.

Jason walked out of the police station feeling totally helpless. He got in his car and headed for the Higgins house. He dreaded having to tell Shirley and Tom that he didn't know for sure where Andrea was, but what he dreaded even more, was telling them what he suspected. The drive back felt extremely long.

Entering the house, he could hear the Higgins family talking in the living room. Jason paused to gather his thoughts before entering. Shaking his head, he sat down as the family looked to him. With everyone's eyes upon him, he shook his head indicating that what he was about to tell them was definitely not good news.

"I'm at a loss. I just don't know what to do. Alex seems to be winning this one I'm afraid. I know he's taken her someplace. Most likely she's in that house. Yes, Cindy has been in on it all along. I went to the police and told them what I suspected. Legally, they can't help. She hasn't been missing long enough for them to do anything. And if Alex has taken her to his place, I'm afraid of what that might do to her. If she gets flashbacks of what really happened to her in her childhood . . . I'm not so sure she will be able to handle it," he said wearily.

"Please tell me it isn't true. He can't be the same Alex Longred!" Shirley said as she started crying. She was hoping it wasn't.

"I'm afraid so," Tom said. "And I agree with Jason. You know how bad she was when she was little. I don't think we have anything to worry about in regards to Alex figuring things out. He seems too obsessed with himself."

Shirley began crying harder, "What if . . . if she can't handle it. I can't bear to think of what'll happen to her?"

"Now, Shirley," Tom said as he put his arm around her, "take it easy. We don't know for certain that she is really in that house. If she is, maybe she's stronger then we think and will be able to handle it."

Jason stood up. "I've got to do something. George, Daniel, I need you come with me. If there's a way to get into that house, we're going to find it. If not, we're just gonna bust the front door down again and head straight in," Jason said determinedly.

"I'm coming too," Tom said grabbing his coat and heading towards the door.

"No" Jason said. "You stay here. It's nearly morning and you're both extremely tired. Shirley needs your support right now. I'm afraid you're both going to need all your strength when we bring Andrea back. I have no idea what shape she'll be in, mentally or physically. You'll need to be prepared for the worst and if there's trouble, you shouldn't be involved."

"I suppose you're right," Tom said. And with that decided, the brave young men left. Shirley and Tom could do nothing but wait and pray for everything to turn out all right.

Meanwhile, Alex and his gang rehung the front door that Jason had knocked down. They made sure the door would be easily kicked open making it easy for Jason to enter the house. Easy entry for Jason fit in with their plans for Jason's return. They had decided that when Jason returned they'd let him get inside the house and get almost to the attic before they made their moves. They were sure Jason would assume they were keeping Andrea in the attic. Then, they would lock him up with Andrea and take care of business with her right before his eyes. Taking their positions about the house, they waited for Jason's inevitable return.

Jason, George and Daniel drove as fast as possible to get to Alex's house before sunrise. On the way, they discussed how to handle the situation.

During the conversation, George asked Jason "What's this all about? Why'd mom get so upset when she found out where Alex lived?"

Daniel also questioned Jason "Why is everyone talking in riddles about Andrea as a little girl?"

Refusing to answer their questions, Jason said "You need to ask your parents and that's all I'm going to tell you." He didn't know how much they wanted their sons to know.

As they approached the driveway to Alex's house, they turned the car lights off. Driving only halfway up the driveway they parked their car behind a large group of trees. The sun would be rising soon and they didn't want anyone to see them. They needed the element of surprise.

Quickly and quietly they snuck up to the house. Splitting up, they went in opposite directions around the house, with Jason exploring the rear. Jason soon found an open window to the basement and crawled in. As he hit the floor, he stood very still and listened. He couldn't hear anything. He waited a couple of minutes for his eyes to adjust to the darkness. Now he could see where he was going. Where would Alex keep her, he wondered? As the story went, or as best he could remember, the basement was unfinished. The majority of this basement must be under the main part of the house. Alex wouldn't be dumb enough to hide Andrea where Lance could possibly hear her or accidentally find her. She must be in the other section of the house. The attic! The perfect place, Jason thought. He headed towards the stairs hoping to find Andrea before it was too late. That was, if it wasn't already too late.

George and Daniel were unable to find a way to enter the house. Returning to the front of the house, they waited a few minutes for Jason. When he didn't come back, they stormed the front door assuming that Jason was already inside. Maybe by storming the front door, they'd create enough of a diversion that Jason would be able to find Andrea before Alex realized he was there. Entering the house, they were met by Ed and Dick.

Alex heard the commotion start downstairs, so he and Cindy headed towards the attic. He had to act before Jason. Nearing the door to the attic, they could hear crying. Alex opened the door and couldn't believe his eyes. Cindy gasped. Andrea was facing the door, crying and rocking a fragile old doll carefully in her arms. She looked like a little girl.

Alex continued to stare at her as he pulled out a cigarette and lit it with trembling hands. As he held the match to blow it out, Andrea screamed "Please Alex, please don't burn mommy and daddy up. They love you!"

Alex blew out the match and Andrea started screaming, "Alex get mommy and daddy, the floor hot, ohh . . . too hot for my feet." She climbed onto the top of the trunk.

Alex didn't comprehend what she was talking about. Cindy looked at Alex and then back at Andrea. She couldn't believe what she had just heard. Again she looked at Alex and back at Andrea. Of course! The old folktale about a house burning and the parents of twins dying in the fire. It was true! Alex and Andrea were the twins involved! She could hardly believe it.

"What's she talking about?" Alex asked. "She must be out of her mind."

"I don't think so Alex. I think she knows exactly what she's talking about. I think you're the one who's out of his mind. You two are twins. Can't you see that?" Cindy asked. "Can't you see the resemblance between the two of you?"

"She can't be my twin sister. My sister died when she was four years old. She thinks I burned someone up. I haven't done that. I've done some bad things, but I've never burned anyone up," he said smugly. His mind was spinning as he sat down.

"And you, you'll have to forget everything that you've just heard and I do mean everything!" he yelled.

From somewhere behind him, Jason said, "I don't think she'll forget a thing. That is, unless she wants to be an accessory to kidnapping or even worse, murder. You don't want that now do you, Cindy?" Jason said as he sneered at Alex.

Cindy stepped back. Her mind was racing. Things were happening too fast. At this point Alex decided it was time to take care of Jason once and for all. Alex stood up and pulled out a gun and pointed it towards Jason.

"This time I'm going to kill you!" he stated.

Jason carefully eyed the situation. If he could get close enough, he'd be able to get the gun away from Alex.

"What good would killing me do?" Jason said as he inched his way forward. "Cindy would know everything, so you'd have to kill her too. Don't you think three missing people would cause suspicion by the police? They'd start searching for us and eventually the investigation would lead here. Especially since at least a half a dozen people know that Cindy and I are here tonight, including the police," he said as he kept inching forward. He had to keep Alex talking. He still needed a couple more seconds to get close enough.

"Besides, just how long have you known that you were the one who killed your parents?" Jason asked. The more confused he got him, the better his chances were for getting the gun away from him.

Alex stood aiming the gun at Jason and getting more and more bewildered by the minute. "I . . . but . . . I didn't kill my parents. A fire did" Alex said.

"But you started the fire, Alex. You wanted your parents dead. You purposely set their bedroom on fire while they were sleeping. Then you brought Andrea up here to the attic telling her that the two of you were going to play a new game," Jason said as he continued to move closer and closer.

Cindy was watching Jason and finally realized what he was trying to do. She nodded at Jason and gave Alex a shove. Jason sprang on Alex and tried to grab the gun. The gun went off as they fell to the floor. Cindy watched horrified as Jason slowly stood up holding the gun and left Alex lying on the floor with his shoulder bleeding badly.

"Call the police," Jason told Cindy, as he motioned for her to go downstairs.

As she turned towards the stairs, Ed, Joe and Dick appeared. They had heard the gun shot and came running. Right behind them, were George and Daniel.

"You're not going anywhere," Joe said as he grabbed her wrists.

"Let her pass through fellows, or you'll wind up like him," Jason stated as he pointed Alex's gun towards them.

Joe let go of Cindy's wrists and she ran down the stairs. Joe, Ed, and Dick figured it was all over.

"George, get over here and watch him," Jason said handing him the gun. Pointing to the rope that had been used to tie up Cindy and Andrea, Jason said, "Daniel use that rope to tie all of them up."

"Where's Andrea?" Daniel asked. Hearing crying he turned around and saw her. "Oh my God!" was all he could say.

Jason quickly ran to her wrapping his arms around her. Pulling her close to him he began stroking her hair saying, "There, there now, my Andrea. Everything is going to be all right. It's going to be all right." But Jason wondered whether everything would ever be all right again.

It had taken only a few minutes for the police to arrive, since a patrol car was in the area as they said it would be. They waited for Cindy to escort the officers to the attic. As they entered, Cindy began explaining what had taken place. Jason added bits of information where it was needed. He let Cindy do the explaining, and he let her leave out the parts where she had been helping Alex to keep Andrea here. The police handcuffed Alex, called an ambulance for him and led the rest of his gang down the stairs to the patrol car. They asked Cindy to come to the station and make a statement regarding her and Andrea's kidnappings, the robbing of the drug store, and about the plot to eventually kill Jason and Andrea. As the police were taking Alex away, one of the officers stayed behind and asked Jason, "What about her?" as he pointed to Andrea. "Shall I call an ambulance for her also?" He sounded very concerned.

"No, I'm going to take her home where she belongs" Jason said shaking his head.

"All right" the officer said. "We'll be in touch with you later. There are a lot of questions which you're going to have to answer for us." Then he left.

George and Daniel walked over to Andrea and Jason. You could see the tears in their eyes as they watched their sister and wondered what had happened to make her like this.

"Come on Jason," George finally said, "Let's get her out of here and home." They helped Jason get Andrea on her feet.

She was still mumbling, "Alex, bad boy, he must be punished, mommy and daddy will punish. Ohhh . . . floor is so hot." She kept picking up her feet as they headed towards the stairs. They carried her down to the main floor. Daniel ran ahead and brought their car up to the front door. Jason put Andrea in the back seat and got in with her. George and Daniel got in the front with George in the driver's seat.

"George," Daniel asked, "Do you know what's going?"

"No, I don't and Jason's too preoccupied right now to answer our questions. After we get her home and she's seen the doctor, maybe mom and dad will fill us in. Then hopefully we'll be able to help her," George said quietly.

"Jason you all right?" Daniel asked turning towards the back seat so he could see Jason.

"I'll be fine," he said as he choked on his words. My lovely Andrea, he thought, will you ever be the same? Will you ever come out of this? He prayed, "Oh, please dear God, let her come out of this so I can show her how much I love her. So that we . . . the two of us can be together. Oh please dear God, I've wasted so much time already."

After what seemed like an eternity to Jason they pulled into the driveway of their home a couple hours past sunrise. Tom and Shirley came running out of the house. They'd sat up all night waiting for them.

"Daniel, George," Jason said quickly, "get your mother back into the house where she won't be able see Andrea. She shouldn't see her like this, not just yet anyway. I don't think she'll be able to handle this. Your father and I will get her to her room, settle her in and, hopefully, calm her down. Then your father can prepare your mother for what to expect when she finally sees her" he ordered.

"Okay" George said as they both hopped out of the car. They didn't question Jason's request.

"Mom, come on back in the house with us," Daniel said as he placed his arms around her and simultaneously spinning her around heading her back towards the house.

"But I want to see Andrea," Shirley said, trying to turn around again but Daniel wouldn't let her.

"Let Jason and dad get her up to her room. Then you can see her," George said.

"Now calm down and come with us. We can't have you getting upset too," Daniel said.

"Upset . . . is she just upset?" Shirley asked looking at Daniel and then at George hoping he was telling her the truth.

"Well, sort of," George said. "For now, let dad and Jason take care of her," and they entered the house leading their mother to the parlor where she wouldn't be able to see Jason and Tom taking Andrea up to her room. When they entered the house, Marabel was waiting for them.

"Marabel would you please fix mom some hot tea and bring us some coffee?" Daniel asked.

Marabel nodded and turned back towards the kitchen.

Running to the car, Tom opened Andrea's door saying, "I'm so glad you're all right. Here let me help you out of the car," and then he heard her mumbling and crying, 'Alex . . . fire . . . punish . . . mommy . . . daddy.'

"Oh no! What happened?" Tom asked almost unable to get the words out.

"I guess from being in that house, and of all places . . . the attic . . . is where Alex put her. It appears being there has brought back all of the memories, the bad memories of her past. The ones we had hoped to keep

99

from her forever. Apparently they made her go into shock," Jason said.

"You know the whole story about her past?" Tom asked surprisingly.

"Yeah, Shirley told me a few years ago when Andrea said something about her past that neither I nor Andrea understood. After Andrea left the room, I asked Shirley just what Andrea had been talking about. It was obvious to me that Shirley knew exactly what she had meant, but didn't want to tell Andrea. She thought it best that I know since I keep such a close eye on her. Right now I think she's remembering too much too fast," Jason said with much concern.

"Let's get her upstairs and into bed. I'll call Dr. Thor and have him come over at once," Tom said. They carried her upstairs. After helping Jason get her in bed, Tom went into the study to call Dr. Thor. He would be able to help her if anyone could. He was the physician who had taken care of her before. Then he went to talk with his wife. He was going to have to prepare her for this.

Jason stayed with Andrea. He didn't want her to be left alone, nor did he want to leave her side. He so desperately wanted to be able to help her.

Tom entered the parlor. Shirley rose quickly and went over to him.

"Your sons keep stopping me from going up to see Andrea. Will you please tell them it's okay to let me go to her?" Shirley demanded.

"I don't think that's such a good idea. Not just yet. You see, honey, I've called Dr. Thor and asked him to come right over and take a look at her . . . she's . . . in a state of shock right now. Maybe after he has examined her, you can go up, but right now, let Jason sit with her. He'll take good care of her," Tom said as he lead Shirley back to her chair.

"No he won't!" Shirley said. "He left her alone last night. He can't be trusted." Shirley said purely out of anguish. She didn't mean a word of what she said.

"Now Shirley," Tom said "you don't mean that and you know it. If it wasn't for Jason, she wouldn't be here at home right now. She'd still be in the hands of Alex."

"You're right," Shirley said, "it's just that I'm so worried about her."

"I know" Tom said, "I know."

"Here drink the rest of your tea while we wait for Dr. Thor," Tom added, but he was so upset he couldn't sit still himself. He kept getting up and walking about the room.

"Dad," Daniel finally said, "I know it's probably not the best time to ask you this, but just what's going on with Andrea? We haven't the slightest idea of what's happening to her."

Tom decided that after everything that had happened, he had no other choice but to tell his sons the complete story. After all they had gone to help rescue her. He felt he owned them that much.

"I don't know where to begin . . . I don't know if I can. But, I'll try. You see . . . when you were all very young you had an aunt and uncle who used to come over quite often. Do you remember them at all?" he asked.

"Vaguely," George said.

"Not really," Daniel added.

"Just as well," Tom said. "Shirley would you rather we go into the study to discuss this? I don't want to upset you anymore?"

"No, I'll be fine. Go ahead," she said as she sipped her tea.

Daniel and George looked at each other. What could possibly be so bad that it would upset their mother more than she already was.

"Well, you see, I had a younger sister named Sandra. She married a very nice young man named Harry." Tom

101

paused for what seemed like a very long time. "His name was Harry . . . Harry Longred."

"That's Alex's last name" George said surprised.

"You can't mean the same family?" Daniel asked.

"Yes, I can. Harry and Sandra were Alex's parents," Tom stated turning to look out the window.

Daniel and George began to ask more questions, but Tom interrupted them.

"Please, just let me tell you the story in its' proper sequence. It should answer most of your questions. Harry was a very wealthy man. He had no family in this country. For that matter, Harry only knew of one distant living relative. He lived in England and his name was Lance. Yes, the Lance that is the guardian of Alex. When Harry got engaged to Sandra, he made our family his family. They married and we became quite . . . close. Sandra soon became pregnant. Everyone was delighted at the thought of them becoming parents. After all, we already had both of you. We had a complete family and Harry wanted so much to have a family of his own. Anyway, when Sandra's time came, she delivered twins."

Again Tom paused. "She had a boy and a girl. They named them Alex and Andrea. Those were also the names of Harry's parents."

George tried to interrupt, but Tom continued on.

"Everything was going along fine for them. Harry continued to thrive in his business and we continued to go on family outings together, but everyone soon learned to keep a watchful eye on Alex. He always seemed a little different from everyone else, if you know what I mean. He also seemed to really enjoy fire. Now, everyone enjoys fires, but his interest in fire was very unusual. He was truly mesmerized by the flames. This fact made Sandra very uncomfortable. One day she came to me quite upset. She had caught Alex burning down one of their old woodsheds. She said that as he watched it burn he had a strange gleam in his eyes. It had really frightened her.

We talked about it and she felt a little better about it, but it still caused her concern. Anyway, everything seemed to be going along fine for them until that . . . that awful day."

Daniel started to say something, but this time Shirley nodded her head no, so he remained silent.

Tom slumped down in the chair. He just couldn't seem to continue telling the story. It was much, much too painful for him.

Shirley rose and went over to him and placed an arm about his shoulders, and continued for him.

"It was very early in the morning when the house caught fire. Sandra and Harry were still asleep. By the time anyone realized that the house was on fire, there was absolutely no way to save Sandra and Harry. You see, the fire had been started in their bedroom. The investigation afterwards showed that it had been deliberately set. It wasn't an electrical fire or anything like that. We don't know if Sandra and Harry ever woke up that morning to find their bedroom on fire. We hope for their sakes, they didn't. Anyway, the firemen found Alex and Andrea up in the attic. Andrea was in a state of shock. Much like the one your father says she appears to be in now. Everyone who knew anything about Alex, always believed he had deliberately set his parents' bedroom on fire and the few facts the investigators had, all pointed towards Alex. Why? No one knows. Only Alex could answer that question, and he was only four years old. What could he possibly tell you? Andrea wasn't much help to them either. When she was found in the attic, all she could do was mumble a few words. All of them were about Alex and a fire and then she stopped talking completely."

Tom had composed himself enough by now that he could finish telling the story.

"So we adopted Andrea and let it be known that no one in town was to tell our children, nor their children

103

about us adopting her or talk about the incident in anyway. We wanted her to think of us as her real parents in hopes that she would be able to forget the past. Forever. We didn't want anyone else to speak of it for fear that someone would eventually tell her. You see, when we were finally able to bring her home from the hospital, she wasn't able to talk, would hardly eat, and in the middle of the night she would wake up screaming her head off. Yet she still couldn't express to us what she was feeling," Tom paused again.

"Then one day she just started talking. Her mind had finally accomplished the only thing that it was able to handle, which was to completely block out everything that had happened to her. The one thing we didn't plan on was that Alex would ever cross paths with her," Tom stated.

Tom rose and walked over to the window again. "You see, we just couldn't adopt him feeling that he had killed my very own sister, so we wrote to Harry's uncle Lance in England. We asked him to please send for Alex and have him come live with him in England. Instead, Lance saw this as an opportunity for him to come live in America. He sold his house in England, packed up his belongings and came to live in Sandra and Harry's old house. Yes, that's the house Alex now lives in. Lance had to have extensive repairs done to the house. He had it fixed up exactly as the house was before the fire. I've only been in that house once since that awful day. Your mother and I have lived in fear of this happening ever since. We were afraid Andrea was still mentally unable to handle what had happened to her in that house." Tom finished and turned around to look at Daniel and George.

Both were at a loss for words.

"For what it's worth," Tom added, "Andrea is a mirror image of Sandra. A real beauty. She's even acquired Sandra's natural elegance and grace. Sometimes when I see her coming down the stairs, I have to do a double take because I think I'm seeing my sister Sandra" he said as he started to get choked up. He sat down and pounded his fist on the table feeling regret at what the past had done to Andrea, his sister, and both families.

"Alex has to pay this time. He has to pay," Tom added in anguish.

Finally the doorbell rang. It was Dr. Thor. Tom let him in and escorted him up to Andrea's room.

To Daniel and George, it seemed like a lifetime had just passed before them. They finally learned why Andrea remembered things they couldn't. Why there were no pictures, or why they had no memories, of her as a baby. Now they knew. They were almost in a state of shock themselves.

Chapter Seven

Jason rose as Dr. Thor and Tom entered Andrea's room.

"You'll have to leave now, Jason," Dr. Thor said. "You may return when I finish examining her. You too, Tom. Just go downstairs and wait for me. You've given me enough information about the situation as you led me up here. Now both of you go," he said as he closed the door behind them.

Dr. Thor took out his instruments and began examining Andrea. He didn't like what he was seeing at all. For one thing, he couldn't pry the doll out of her arms. That wasn't a good sign. After completing his examination, he went downstairs to the anxiously awaiting family. He dreaded having to give them the results.

Entering the parlor, he put his bag on the table behind the sofa. Then he walked around in front of the sofa to face Tom and Shirley squarely. "She's in a state of shock as I'm sure you are aware," he said. "I have sedated her. It should help her sleep comfortably for a while."

"Will she be all right?" Shirley asked with tears in her eyes. Even though she hadn't yet seen her daughter, she knew just how bad she was. She could sense it and she remembered all too well how bad she was the first time.

"I don't know. Not just yet anyway," he said. "She's in pretty bad shape. She may never recover from this, or she may pull through in an hour, a week or who knows. At this point, everything is really up to her and how strong her spirit to live is. We all know she has a strong will to live. She's proven that to us once already in her young life."

"May I go up and see her now?" Shirley asked the doctor.

"Yes, but I'd advise not staying too long. If she wakes up and becomes hysterical, call me and I'll give her another sedative. We'll just have to go that route for a while and see how she reacts." Dr. Thor gathered his things, and just before he left he said he'd be stopping by again the next morning.

Shirley quickly thanked Dr. Thor and headed up the stairs before Tom had a chance to stop her. As Shirley entered Andrea's room, she was crying softly. Shirley sat down and started rubbing Andrea's forehead while watching her sleep.

Shirley sat beside Andrea for nearly four hours when she heard the doorbell ring downstairs. A few moments later, Tom entered the room.

"Shirley, honey," he said, "the police are here. We have to sign a complaint to press charges against Alex and his gang," he added looking at her wearily.

Reluctantly she rose and headed downstairs.

"How can we press charges against . . . against her very own brother?" Shirley said as she started crying again when she saw the waiting police officers.

"Now Shirley," Tom said. "I can't see how we can do anything else. There will be a trial and hopefully they'll place him in a mental institution. That's where he belongs. Andrea is in no condition to press charges against him herself. We must do this for her . . . and for Alex. Andrea would want us to help him. It's the best thing we can do for him," Tom said as he placed his arms around Shirley's shaking shoulders.

"Excuse me folks," the police officer said. "I don't understand . . . Andrea is your daughter and yet you say Alex is her brother?"

"Yes," Tom said. "Let me explain. You see we adopted Andrea when she was four years old. We didn't adopt her twin brother, Alex. Their parents were killed in a fire in their own home. Everyone assumed that Alex set the fire, but no one could prove it. If you check the records of the Osceola County Police Department, you'll see that this was the conclusion of the investigation done by their office. We never told Andrea she was adopted or that she had a twin brother. When we adopted her, she could hardly talk, and we thought it best not to tell her about her past. When Alex kidnapped her, he took her back to the house where they grew up and he put her in the attic. Being back in that house brought back all the memories of what had happened to her, which she had tried so hard to forget when she was little."

"I'm sorry, Mr. Higgins, I had no idea," the officer said. "I'm sure with all the surrounding circumstances and your testimonies, Alex will have a good chance of being placed in a mental institution."

George and Daniel were still reeling from what they had learned. Listening to their father retell the story, they still found it hard to believe. They were astonished that they had never heard anyone speak of it. They knew their father was a man of great influence and power in this town, but they were just now beginning to realize how powerful he really was.

"Mrs. Higgins, if you'll please sign here," the officer said, "and Mr. Higgins here, we'll be on our way and leave you to tend to your daughter," he said as they signed the paper. "There, that takes care of it. I certainly hope your daughter pulls through this. One more question, do you know where I can find Jason Steele? We have some further questions for him."

"Right here officer" Jason said as he walked out of the study.

"Jason, have you been sitting in there by yourself all this time?" Shirley asked concerned.

"Yes. I've been doing some thinking. But right now, if you don't mind, may we use the study to discuss the matter at hand?" Jason asked as he gestured for the officers to go into the study.

"Of course," Tom said. "Take all the time you need."

Jason and the officers went into the study and closed the door behind them.

"Is Jason in any trouble?" Shirley asked while looking at Tom.

"No, I'm sure he's not. The police need him to verify the story Cindy gave them. I'm sure that's all it is," Tom said wondering whether there was more to the story than Jason had said.

Shirley headed towards the parlor. On the way she asked Marabel to fix some sandwiches for everyone. She was sure no one was hungry, but she knew they needed to eat to keep up their strength. She was starting to get weary herself. After all, they'd been up all night. Shirley was hesitant to leave Andrea alone in her room but she needed to rest for a while and Andrea wasn't going to wake up soon anyway.

Jason and the officers were in the study for nearly three hours discussing the events that had taken place. When the officers finished with Jason, they told him they doubted Alex would ever have a chance of coming back out into the free world again. As Jason led the officers towards the front door, the officers told him to stay available in case they needed more information from him. Jason said he would and then headed for Andrea's room.

Andrea was still asleep. He sat down on her bed and took her hand, and with tears in his eyes said, "Andrea, please pull out of this, I need you . . . I love you . . . please Andrea. I'll show you just how much I love you if you'll please . . . just pull out of this." Jason heard the door behind him close. As he turned to look, there stood Tom.

"Jason," he said, "I'm sorry but I heard every word you just said and well . . . I must confess I've known for a long time now just how much you love Andrea. Believe

109

me the same goes for her. Though she has never said so, I've seen it in her eyes and in her actions, too."

"She's just got to pull through this. It's all my fault anyway. If I hadn't left with Sheryl at the party, she wouldn't have gone with Ted. None of this would have happened," Jason said as he started to get choked up.

"Now, Jason, you can't blame yourself. This would have eventually happened one way or another. Alex was determined to get to her. If it hadn't happened last night, it would have happened another time. Remember Cindy was also helping him. If Andrea had been at the ball, she would have gone with Cindy to see what she wanted. If Cindy had said she wanted to talk with Andrea alone, she would have told you to get lost. Cindy and Alex would have gotten her anyway," Tom said reassuringly.

"I guess you're right. I wouldn't have been able to stop him from getting to her unless I had kept her in a cage, and she's too free a spirit to have that done to her . . . or at least she was," Jason said.

"I know," Tom said placing a hand on Jason's shoulder. "I want her to pull though this too."

"I'm sorry. Here I am feeling sorry for myself, when you must feel just as bad as I do, or worse," Jason said as he tried to get control of himself once again.

Andrea started to toss her head back and forth. As she did so she dropped the doll she had been holding on to for so long.

Tom grabbed her hand. "Andrea, can you hear me? Andrea . . . Andrea can you hear me?"

Andrea's eyes opened. She slowly looked around the room then stared at Jason for a long time, then switched to stare at her father.

"Andrea, sweetheart, do you understand me?" Tom asked again, but Andrea just stared at him with a blank look on her face. "Andrea, please," but she just turned her head away from him.

"Please say something, please show me that you know we're here," Jason begged as he moved to where she could see him. Andrea continued to stare off into space without so much as the blinking of an eyelash.

With tears in his eyes, Jason left the room. Andrea couldn't or wouldn't speak. Could things get any worse?

Shirley and Marabel were coming up the stairs with hot soup for Andrea. Seeing Jason standing outside her room, Marabel said "Is she awake yet? I've got some nice hot soup for her," as she remembered the day they had brought Andrea home the first time.

"She's awake," Jason said looking down at the floor. "But . . . she . . . won't talk. She won't acknowledge if she knows anyone is even in the room."

Shirley took the soup and went into the room. Marabel led Jason downstairs. He looked as though he was falling apart. Marabel had to pull him back together again. That was her specialty.

Tom was still holding onto Andrea's hand when Shirley entered with the soup.

"Hello Andrea," Shirley said. "Look what I've brought you, your favorite soup. I'm sure you must be starving by now," she said setting the tray down beside her bed. Tom shook his head and moved away. Again Andrea didn't acknowledge that she knew Tom had let go of her hand, moved away, nor that her mother was beside her. Shirley raised the spoon full of soup to Andrea's lips, but she couldn't open her mouth. Shirley tried to pry Andrea's mouth open and force her to eat but she couldn't budge it. Andrea was not about to eat anything.

"Andrea," Tom said as he took her hand once more, "if you know we're here, please just squeeze my hand." Andrea just laid there. He tried again. But still no response. They left with tears in their eyes. When they got downstairs, they found the whole family still sitting in the living room.

111

"Call Dr. Thor," Shirley said to Tom. "He needs to be made aware of this new complication."

Tom walked out and called Dr. Thor from the study. Dr. Thor said he would be over as quickly as possible. Sitting quietly, they waited for his return. Jason let him in and walked him to Andrea's room. Then he returned to the living room to wait with the rest of the family.

After an hour or so, Dr. Thor walked into the living room to talk with the family after re-examining Andrea.

"How bad is she?" Tom questioned. He was afraid the worst of his fears were now coming true.

"It's pretty bad," the doctor said shaking his head. "I'm afraid her mind has paralyzed her entire body. She can't even move her little toe, nor does she seem to have feeling anywhere on her body. She can't open her mouth or at least it seems her mind won't let her. The only movement she has is being able to move her head from side to side. She appears to be in a coma like state. I just don't know what I can tell you. If she continues at this rate for more than a month, I'm afraid there won't be much hope of her ever coming out of it. We're going to have to start feeding her intravenously immediately. I'd like to hospitalize her," he added.

Shirley jumped up immediately and said "No! We can care for her here. I want her to be around familiar surroundings. I don't want her in a hospital."

"All right. I'll arrange to have a nurse come over immediately with everything Andrea's going to need. The nurse can stay here with her," he said.

"No, we'll do whatever she needs done," Shirley stated.

"Of course," Dr. Thor said. He could tell Shirley was very upset and he knew she thought she was doing what was best for her. He wouldn't disagree with her for now. He knew her emotions were high. "The nurse can teach you how to do everything she's going to need done. I won't push the issue of hospitalizing her for now. But, if her condition worsens in any way, if that's possible, I will insist."

"Of course," Tom said as he came to stand by Dr. Thor. "We only want to do what's best. We'll do whatever you say."

"Maybe keeping her here around familiar surroundings will help bring her back to reality. It might be our only hope. With all of your help, hopefully, she will pull through this. Andrea's going to need an I-V and she's going to need her arms and legs exercised everyday to keep her joints from stiffing up. Hopefully it will also slow the atrophying process. If this goes on for very long walking again will be very hard for her." Dr. Thor continued. "The mind can be and is a very powerful force. It can kill the body and, that seems to be what her mind wishes to do. There's nothing I can do to help pull her out of this except for the obvious. It might be wise if someone sits with her at all times to see if she shows any signs of improvement. If we can find one small spark to start with, maybe we'll able to use it to our advantage. Without a starting place, I'm stumped."

"Now I'll go call my office and get everything under way. I could have one of my nurse's stay with her as I said. Are you sure you don't want that?" he asked.

"No, that won't be necessary. We'll manage just fine, but thank you for your kind offer," Shirley added.

"Fine, now where is a phone I may use?" Dr. Thor asked.

"Right this way," Shirley said as she led him to the study. After consulting with his office, he returned to the living room to pick up his belongings.

"I'll stop in once a day to see how she is doing and to check on the I-V's I'm having started in her arm," he said as he continued to gather his things. He shook his head and said to Shirley and Tom "I'm sorry, so very sorry. She's such a wonderful girl," and with that he left.

113

The whole family was stunned. Could it be possible that she might not make it? No one would or could believe they might lose her. They wouldn't accept the fact that Andrea could possibly die.

"While we wait for the nurse to arrive, I'll take the first shift of sitting with her," George said heading to Andrea's room.

Soon the nurse arrived bringing everything she needed to begin Andrea's treatment. Shirley showed her to Andrea's room.

"It'll only take me a few minutes to set everything up. Why don't you ask everyone to come up here in about 15 minutes. I should be ready to demonstrate how to change the I-V bags by then," she directed.

"I'll go get everyone," George said.

Shirley stayed. She wanted to watch what the nurse was doing. She wanted to see how to set up the pole and how to start the I-V. She knew she wasn't going to have to put the I-V in, but she wanted to know how just in case. Finally, everyone came into Andrea's room. They stood quietly watching Andrea.

Before she began, she waited a few moments to give the family time to adjust to seeing Andrea in such a state. She showed them how to change the I-V bag and instructed them to watch it very carefully.

"Always be aware of the level of fluid in the bag. The bag should never run out. If the bag runs out and isn't changed quickly enough, blood would start to back up in the I-V tube and could cause Andrea harm" the nurse stated. Then she showed them were the full bags of fluid where kept and how to make sure they remained sterile. After giving them a checklist of what to do and what to look for as it related to the I-V, she began instructions on how to exercise her arms and her legs. She also indicated that they should talk to her as much as possible and read to her.

"When patients are in state like this, we aren't sure if they can hear us but doctors feel it best if you keep talking and reading to them to help stimulate the brain," the nurse stated.

Then she added "Tell her stories about things you've done together in the past. Include what she did and use colorful descriptions of what everything looked like."

It appeared to be a daunting task waiting before them. They knew they had to do it. They all wanted to do it. They just hoped it would help bring Andrea back to them.

"Does anyone have any questions?" the nurse asked. No one said anything. She put her card right next to the phone in Andrea's room.

"Call me day or night if you have questions or if you feel Andrea is getting worse" she said. Then she left.

Jason slowly left Andrea's room. He suddenly felt drained of all his strength. What would he do if he lost her? It was going to be one long evening for him, and he still hadn't had any sleep. As he entered his house, the last little bit of strength he had drained completely from him. He had to get some rest so he would be able to help Andrea and her family by taking the night shift with her.

As he laid down on his bed he knew he wasn't going to be able to sleep peacefully.

The family kept vigil around the clock, taking turns sitting with Andrea. The first month had come and gone with no change in her condition. Their vigil continued and to everyone's surprise Andrea's condition wasn't getting any worse after another month.

The family had become quite adept in changing her I-V's and bed linens. They even became experts in regulating the I-V. The nurse still stopped by every day to check on Andrea.

The nurse joked with Shirley "I'm beginning to feel I'm not needed anymore. All of you have become so efficient in taking care of everything all of you could get certified as a nurse."

Then the nurse added lightheartedly, "Well, maybe a nurse's aid."

Shirley was so proud of how her family had pulled together to help Andrea.

But Dr. Thor was beginning to get worried about the family. He could see the wear and tear this was having on them, but they didn't see it that way. He pleaded with them to let him put her in an institution where she would have round the clock care. They wouldn't hear of it. He let a couple more months go by before making his plea again.

"Tom, Shirley" Dr. Thor started "I don't see how you can keep this up. It's not doing any of you any good. You're all getting very tired. Her condition hasn't changed since she came home. My diagnosis is that her condition will eventually begin to get worse. This could go on for months or years. Are you willing to keep this up for that long? Won't you please consider placing her where she can get round the clock care and you can get some rest?"

"Absolutely not!" Shirley stated. "We're going to keep her here. I know having her here is the best thing for her. I don't care what it does to us. We're going to take care of her. We're not going to put her in an institution and that's final" she declared.

Dr. Thor relented. He was sure that eventually they would agree with him. With the holidays coming, he understood why Tom and Shirley wanted Andrea at home. He'd try again after the holidays.

Shirley and Tom walked into the parlor after their exchange with Dr. Thor.

"You know Shirley," Tom said looking at her. "We may have to consider Dr. Thor's proposal. I don't like the thought of it either, but this could go on for months or even years. You've heard of cases like this. It's depressing but, it's something I think we're going to have to consider," he said as he sat down close to her.

"Christmas will be here soon and I can't bear the thought of Christmas without her. I know she won't be able to be down here with us, but at least she'll be in this house. We're doing okay aren't' we? We have to continue doing what we're doing. I can't give up on her," Shirley said wearily.

"I'm not giving up on her. I just think we need to consider all possibilities," he said. He knew Shirley wouldn't change her mind and in his heart he didn't want Andrea anywhere but home.

Chapter Eight

It was closing in on Christmas and the family had many misgivings about the upcoming holiday season. They didn't feel like decorating the house or buying Christmas gifts, but Shirley kept pushing them to go about their usual Christmas rituals. Christmas was Andrea's favorite time of year and she knew Andrea would want them to go all out for Christmas, just like they did every year.

Daniel and George finally decorated the outside of the house, making it look especially festive even though their hearts weren't in it.

Shirley decorated the inside of the house, placing the Christmas tree in the living room. They usually put up an artificial tree but since Andrea always wanted a real tree, they bought a real one and decorated it. Shirley secretly wished she had granted Andrea's request before this terrible thing happened. Maybe this year if they had a real tree, Andrea might come out of a coma and be able to see it. They picked out a big beautiful tree that filled the room with the wonderful scent of pine.

Slowly, the family began placing presents under the Christmas tree, even though they didn't feel right doing so with Andrea lying in her bed in her paralyzed state.

One morning as Shirley was cleaning Andrea's room and straightening out her closet, she noticed a big bag tucked way back in the corner. Opening the bag she thought she saw presents. "What's this?" she wondered. Shirley reached in the bag and pulled them out. They were Christmas presents. Each one had been wrapped in Christmas paper and had a nametag on it. She wondered why Andrea had done some of her Christmas shopping for the next year so early in the year. She always did do her Christmas shopping early, but in the spring? That was very strange but since she had the presents, she was going to put them under the tree for the family to open on Christmas morning.

Shirley walked over to Andrea and took her hand, "What's going on in that mind of yours Andrea? Why did you buy Christmas presents so early? Did you know something was going to happen to you? Did you have a premonition of something? Oh probably not, you just love Christmas so much you got an early start. You probably planned on buying more than this didn't you? This was just a head start right?" Shirley asked rubbing Andrea's forehead. She got up from the bed, picked up the presents and headed for the Christmas tree. She wanted to put them under the tree before anyone in the family saw them.

The family awoke on Christmas morning to snowflakes gently falling. As Shirley looked out her window, she was remembering how Andrea always hoped it would snow on Christmas. To her, the snowfall made the day more festive. Remembering Andrea's excitement of Christmas's in the past, Shirley's eyes swelled with tears.

"Let's go downstairs. I'm sure everyone has already gathered in the living room. I heard George get up and go downstairs quite some time ago," Tom said.

"All right," Shirley said dabbing away the tears with her handkerchief.

It was tradition for the Higgins family to gather in the living room early on Christmas morning before breakfast to exchange gifts. Jason was always included. As they entered the living room, sure enough, everyone was there. Everyone, that is except for Andrea. They sat quietly for a while.

Finally Daniel asked, "Mom, shall we open our gifts now, or should we wait until Andrea is able to join us?"

"No, no, she wouldn't want us to wait. She never was one who could wait very long on Christmas morning to open presents and you know how strongly she feels about Christmas," Shirley said. "It's got to be a big production and always celebrated at the appropriate time on the appropriate day," she added as her eyes teared up again. She leaned back on the couch.

"First though," Tom said, "I think we each should say a silent prayer. Then open our gifts. If God's going to grant us a miracle, today's a perfect day for one." He took Shirley's hand and bowing their heads, each said their own private prayer. They knew they all had prayed for the same thing. Jason himself was choking back the tears.

Jason stood up after getting control of his emotions and said, "I'll play Santa Claus." He remembered what a good Santa Claus Andrea always was. She had a sparkle in her eyes, just as if a little of Santa Claus lived inside her. I have to put on a smile and act happy, he thought. Andrea wouldn't have done it any other way.

"Ho, ho, ho, this one is you . . ." he said as he handed a gift to George, "and this one's for you," as he continued to pass out the presents from underneath their tree until he came to one marked for Andrea.

"This one's . . . for Andrea. I'll just place it here and we'll . . . take all of them up to her later," he said as his voice cracked once more. This was beginning to be much harder than he thought it would be. It became even harder when he saw the gifts that were signed from Andrea. He looked over at Shirley as he began passing them out.

"They really are from Andrea. I found them in her closet the other day. I couldn't believe it. She had actually bought all of these gifts and wrapped them up a long time ago. I think she bought them while she was away at college. She wasn't home long enough before . . . before . . ." She couldn't bring herself to say what had happened to her. "To have done this much shopping," she added.

Everyone was opening their gifts and seemingly enjoying themselves, though there was an undercurrent of sadness amongst them. Jason really liked all the gifts he received. Now he had only one left. Andrea's gift to him. He picked up the gift he had bought for Andrea and the gift she had bought for him and headed up the stairs. He wanted to be in the same room with her when he opened his present from her. The family watched him as he headed for the stairs. They all felt sorry for him. They knew he hurt as much as the rest of them. They thought it would be good to let him have some time alone with her before they all went up.

Jason paused outside Andrea's bedroom door to collect himself, and then opened the door.

"Marabel, I'll stay with her for a while now. You go and have a nice Christmas with your family," he said as he turned towards Andrea.

"Hi sweetheart. I thought I'd open this present with just you. It's the gift you got me. I wonder what it could possibly be? You really surprised us all by having these gifts bought months ago. You're really something," he said as he shook the box and watched her lie there staring off into space. "I brought yours from me up here, too. Here, let's open my gift to you first." He sat down beside her bed and carefully began unwrapping the present.

"Look Andrea, see I wrapped your gift in your favorite wrapping paper. You didn't know I knew what kind of wrapping paper you liked best did you? Let's see now . . ." he said as he held it up for her to see. "Oh, look, it's a diamond necklace. Here, let me place it around your neck." He carefully lifted her head and placed it around her neck. It looked beautiful, but she never even blinked at him. "It looks lovely, Andrea" he said as he watched her, but still no reaction from her. He continued on as if she understood everything.

"I guess it's time for me to open mine," he added. Slowly he unwrapped the present she had bought for him. It was a beautiful diamond ring. He remembered the day he had first seen it. He and Andrea were out running errands for Mrs. Higgins over Andrea's spring break. They went into an antique jewelry store to pick up a pin Shirley was having repaired. While they were waiting for assistance, they were admiring some of the antique jewelry. He casually mentioned to her that he liked this one particular ring. He said he would like to own a ring like that but it was far too expensive for him to justify buying. He didn't think she was paying any attention to what he was saying at the time because she had acted as if she was in a hurry to get going.

"Oh Andrea" he said as he took the ring out and placed it on his finger. Then he took her hand, and quietly watching her, he placed a kiss upon her lips. He knew she didn't feel it, but it made him feel better.

Eventually the whole family gathered in her room and sat down watching her for a while thinking their own private thoughts.

"I have an idea," Daniel said. "You know how Andrea loves to sing those corny Christmas carols . . . well."

"I think that's a great idea," Shirley said.

They gathered closer around her bed and started singing, but one by one they left her room with tears streaming down their cheeks. Christmas day for the Higgins family was not a joyous one.

Jason usually took the night shift of sitting with Andrea. Tonight, even though it was Christmas night, was not going to be any different. As Jason sat quietly with Andrea, Daniel came in.

"Jason, Cindy is downstairs and wants to talk to you," he stated. "She said she'd be waiting for you on the porch of your house. I asked if she wanted to come inside and talk with you here but she said no." Daniel said.

"Thanks," Jason said.

Daniel turned and headed to his bedroom.

He turned to Andrea "I won't be long," he said even though he knew she didn't hear him. Jason headed for his house.

"Hi Jason," Cindy said. "I came by to wish you a Merry Christmas."

Jason stood staring at Cindy. They hadn't seen each other or spoken to each other since the incident except when they had been called to the police station at the same time. They corroborated each other's stories. That had been the extent of contact between them.

"I'm sorry," Cindy said. "I never meant for anything like this to happen to Andrea."

"What do you want Cindy?" Jason asked impatiently. "You certainly didn't come here tonight just to apologize. What is it?"

"No, I thought . . . maybe . . . just maybe, it might be possible for us to patch things up and get back together again?" Cindy replied.

"What! For goodness sake Cindy, be realistic. There never was much between the two of us and there certainly is a lot less now." Jason said angrily. "With Andrea in the state she has been in for all these months, you can't honestly believe that we would ever get back together!" he yelled at her.

Cindy reached for Jason, placing her arms around him. "Please, Jason," Cindy begged. "Look at all I can give you. Andrea can't give you a thing now. If what I hear is true, she'll probably remain like she is for the rest of her life," she said as she pushed her body hard against his.

Jason grabbed her arms and pulled them down. "Don't ever do that again!" he raged. "In fact, I don't ever want to see you again. Now leave before I do something I'll regret!"

With tears in her eyes, Cindy gave Jason a kiss on his cheek, turned and walked away.

Meanwhile . . . Andrea was lying in her bedroom when she began to her noises. Someone was yelling and she saw a flash of faces. A fire and an attic room. Shaking her head, she could still hear yelling. She had to find out who was yelling. She had to get up. She tried to stand, but couldn't. She felt so weak. She tried to pull herself up. She kept trying. She tried to yell for help but was unable to make a sound. What's wrong with me? Why can't I stand up? Why can't I talk? She was confused.

She recognized the voice. It was Jason yelling. He must be in trouble. I've got to help him. I've got to get out of this bed. Finally she got herself upright but fell off her bed. Crawling to the window she pulled the I-V out of her hand. Why do I need an I-V, she wondered? Reaching the window, she saw Jason and Cindy standing on his porch. Cindy kissed him on the cheek, then walked away.

He's not in trouble, she thought. He's just with Cindy. She continued staring out the window, then she began to cry. Jason loves Cindy, she thought, and cried even harder. If he only knew much I love him. She heard her bedroom door open behind her. Turning her head, she saw Jason standing there with a look of shock on his face.

"Andrea!" Jason said running to her, "how . . . why . . . how did you get yourself out of bed?"

Andrea tried to tell him, but nothing would come out. She tried to move her legs, but again she couldn't move them. All she could do was cry. Why can't I walk? Why can't I talk? What's happening to me? Her eyes reflected the terror she was feeling inside.

Jason saw the terror spread over her face and tried to comfort her.

"Andrea, please say something to me," he pleaded as he knelt down in front of her. Waiting a few seconds, he said, "let me go get some help to get you back in bed," and with that he ran out of her room. He was afraid to move her by himself. He didn't want to hurt her in anyway.

"Tom, Shirley, call Dr. Thor," he yelled. "Tell him Andrea's gotten out of bed by herself."

"What?" Tom said as he ran towards Andrea's room.

Without question Shirley ran to the phone and called Dr. Thor. "Dr. Thor I'm sorry to bother you on Christmas, but it seems we have had an unexpected miracle. Andrea has apparently managed to get herself up and out of her bed!" she exclaimed.

Dr. Thor told Shirley he'd be right over.

Shirley quickly went to join the others in Andrea's room. As she entered she saw Andrea sitting by the window crying.

"Andrea honey, how did you get over here?" Tom asked. But once again she was unable to speak or to move about. Tom and Jason carefully picked her up and placed her back in her bed and waited for Dr. Thor.

George waited by the door for the doctor to arrive. When the doctor appeared at the door, George took him directly to Andrea's room.

"Okay everyone, you know the drill. You all have to leave while I examine her. I'll be down directly to fill you in," and he made everyone leave.

After finishing examining Andrea again, he headed back to the parlor to once again to give the family his diagnosis.

"There seems to be little improvement," he said. "But at least there has been a spark. Does anyone know what made her get up in the first place? What was happening at the moment she managed to get up?" he asked.

Everyone was looking at Jason. He finally spoke.

"I don't know . . . I was outside with Cindy. When I returned she was sitting by the window." He was feeling guilty for having left her alone again. Jason sat there trying to think of what could have possibly happened that would have made Andrea go to the window.

"Dr. Thor, could loud noises possibly have triggered something in her brain to make her come out of this shock?" he asked.

"Yes, I suppose so. Why?" Dr. Thor asked.

"Well, I was outside on my porch with Cindy. We were yelling at each other. Could that have been enough of a stimulant?" he asked.

"It's possible. I really don't know," Dr. Thor said.

"That's got to be it," Tom said. "The rest of us were in our own rooms, so the house was quiet. What happened while you were out there?"

"Cindy and I had quite a disagreement that turned into a shouting match. I suppose Andrea could have been able to hear us. That's about it. Oh, there's one more thing. As Cindy was leaving she gave me a goodbye kiss," he added.

"That's probably it," Tom said. "Andrea must have gotten to the window to see what the commotion was all about and saw Cindy kissing you. That would explain her tears. Then she must have gone right back into shock. Jason, please go upstairs and explain everything to her. Explain to her that the kiss didn't mean anything to you. Explain to her that Cindy doesn't mean anything to you anymore too. Please, Jason, it's finally time to let Andrea know how you feel about her. It may be her only hope. Hurry now, go!"

Jason ran up the stairs two at a time and straight into Andrea's room. She was lying there with tears streaming down her face.

"Andrea, darling," Jason said sitting down on her bed and taking both of her hands in his. "From your window did you see Cindy and me on my porch? Please, if you

did, just blink your eyes to let me know you understand."
To Jason's surprise she blinked her eyes at him.

"Sweetheart, listen and listen to very carefully. Cindy
and I are through. Andrea, I love you. I've always loved
you. I always will. I love you," Jason said kissing her
cheek. It felt so good to finally be able to say that directly
to her. Jason sat watching and waiting for a response.

Andrea was lying there thinking too. Could it be true?
Does he really love me? No, not after what I just saw. He
doesn't care about me. He's only telling me this because
there's something wrong with me. Why else would Dr.
Thor have been here examining me? Jason, why are you
torturing me this way? I love you. I really do, but you . . .
why are you trying to hurt me? She wanted to ask him
why, but she couldn't make herself speak no matter now
hard she tried.

Jason was dying inside. Why can't I get through to
her? Why won't she respond? Finally he went back
downstairs.

"Anything?" Shirley asked him but by the look on his
face, she already knew the answer.

Jason shook his head no. He finally said, "She did
acknowledge that she saw Cindy and me. I asked her if
she understood what I was saying to blink her eyes and
she did. But that was all I was able to get from her. I'll go
back up in a little while, but right now I just can't face
her anymore," he said as he sat down placing his face in
his hands.

They sat there hoping to could come up with
something else that would bring her out of this. They'd
been waiting too long for a sign of improvement. They
couldn't give up now.

Some late-night Christmas carolers had arrived at the
Higgns residence and were standing outside their door
and started to sing. Andrea laid in her bed listening to
them. It looks so dark outside it must be close to
midnight, she thought. Christmas must really be close if

there are carolers singing, she thought. If I could just get over to the window again, I could see who is caroling.

Trying to get up again took all of her strength, but she managed to sit up and swing her legs over the edge of the bed. I can do it, she thought. I know I can. I'll get over to the window and watch the carolers for a while. Trying to stand she fell. She pulled herself up and tried again. This time she managed to take a step but fell again. She was getting very angry with herself. She was able to get up again and take a couple of steps. She tried to reach the window seat, but couldn't quite make it. I hear the caroler's voices fading. They're starting to leave. I have to get to the window quick to catch a glimpse of them before they leave. She made it to the window just as the carolers were getting back in their cars to drive away. She sat down completely exhausted and exasperated at herself for not getting to the window quick enough. Why can't I walk? Why did Dr. Thor put this I-V back in my arm? She felt very confused.

As she sat there, she heard her bedroom door open again. Turning around she saw Jason standing there. She was so mad at herself that without even thinking about it she said "You know I'm getting rather tired of you walking into my bedroom anytime you feel like it without knocking. You know I deserve to have some privacy." She thought she was yelling at him but her voice was just a whisper.

Jason started smiling and then laughed out loud as he walked over to her. "You got out of bed again. What made you do it this time? And even though you think you're telling me off, I'm glad you're able to talk again," he said.

"I . . . I don't know," Andrea said softly looking at her legs. "What's wrong with me?"

"Do you remember anything?" he asked. Andrea just shook her head no. Putting his arms around her he lifted her up and said, "You've been very ill for a few months."

Andrea thought nothing of him picking her up and putting her back in bed. She was feeling quite weak and needed his help. Everything was happening to her so fast, she hadn't remembered Jason telling her he loved her, but she was remembering other things. People lifting her arms, legs, and moving her to change the bed sheets. She hadn't been able to move or to speak to any of them. It was like she had been in a dream or a nightmare.

"I . . . I remember something like being sick . . . and Alex and . . . a fire" and she started to crying again.

"Don't try to talk so much. Just sit back in your bed and try to relax. You're not strong enough. I have to go now and tell your parents about you. They're not going to believe this," he said smiling as he turned to leave. Then he stopped and came back to her.

"First, there's something I have to tell you. Something I want to be sure you know before anything else happens to you. Andrea," he said taking her hand and sitting down beside her, "I love you. I know you love me too. I've always felt that you loved me like a brother and not as a companion. Since all this has happened to you, I realized I wouldn't be able to go on without you. Please say you love me, and that you'll . . . you'll do me the honor of becoming my wife. No, don't answer just yet. Please take as much time as you need to think it over. I don't want to rush you into anything. I want to make you my wife, but I want your answer when your mind is clear and you're absolutely certain you want to marry me."

"Jason," Andrea asked hoarsely "What about Cindy?" as she pointed towards her window.

"Ah, yes, you did see us together didn't you? Did you see her kiss me?" he asked.

Andrea nodded her head yes.

"Andrea, as I told Cindy then, and as I am telling you now, their never was anything between Cindy and me because of you. You see, you had already captured my heart. Please believe me Andrea, I love you and only you,"

129

Jason said. After watching her eyes carefully for a few moments, he left to go inform her parents of this new turn of events.

As Jason headed out of the room, Andrea said, "Jason . . . I . . . love you too," but her voice was so weak and hoarse he didn't hear her.

As Jason hurriedly walked towards Shirley and Tom's room, he wondered whether Andrea really believed him. He hadn't been able to tell what she was thinking when he told her he loved her. He just prayed she believed him.

Jason knocked on Tom and Shirley's bedroom door and said, "Get up . . . Andrea's up and talking. Get up everybody! Andrea's up again and I think this time to stay!" he yelled.

Tom came flying out of the room, "What?"

"Come see for yourself!" Jason said as he headed back towards Andrea's room.

Everyone ran into Andrea's. Entering they saw Andrea setting up in bed, alert and obviously moving about.

"Hello mom, hello dad," Andrea said in a whisper as her parents hugged her. Everyone was so excited and talking all at once that no one heard Andrea trying to get Jason's attention. Finally he realized she was trying to talk to him.

"Yes Andrea?" he asked. "What are you trying to say? Everyone, please be still for a moment, I can't hear her." Everyone got quiet as they looked at Jason and Andrea.

Don't they make a handsome couple, Shirley thought.

"Please . . . may I have a moment alone with Jason?" Andrea asked.

"Certainly," Tom said. He was sure he knew what they wanted to talk about.

"Come on you guys, let's go make some coffee and come back in a few minutes," he said, winking at Jason as he herded everyone out of the room.

Andrea patted the bed beside her, "Please sit here," she said to Jason as he sat down and took her hand.

"Are you sure you don't have feelings for Cindy?" she asked staring straight into his eyes as if trying to find some emotion in them. She thought she saw a spark.

Jason saw doubt in her eyes. "Please Andrea, believe me," he said as he placed his hand along side her cheek and staring into her eyes. "I love you. I love you as much as it is humanly possible for a man to love a woman. Even more," as he moved his lips closer to hers. Then he whispered, "I love you," and he kissed her with such passion he found it hard to control himself.

Andrea's response to his kiss was so forceful he could barely believe it. Watching his eyes as he told her he loved her, she finally saw the emotion she had been looking for. It really was true. He really does love me. And now, now he's kissing me. Is this really happening? Or am I still dreaming?

"Jason," she said, "I do . . . love you . . . I have always loved you and yes . . . my mind is crystal clear . . . I . . . want to be your wife more than anything else in this whole wide world."

"Oh darling," he said pulling her towards him, and then the whole family came in as they had heard everything.

Dr. Thor examined Andrea, and was amazed at how quickly she was recovering. He informed the family she needed to take it slow. She needs to remain on liquids for a week and then she can slowly begin eating soft foods. After that, if she feels okay, she can try regular food.

He said she could start talking walks but only a few steps at a time with help. Then, as soon as she felt she was strong enough, she could try walking on her own. Once she mastered taking a few steps on her own, she could go for walks around the bedroom at first. After she could navigate the bedroom all right, then she could try the stairs. He indicated that it was absolutely necessary that this be a gradual process. If she pushed it too quickly, she could damage the muscles in her legs and make her recovery time longer.

Also her brain needed time to adjust as well. It had paralyzed her body for a long time and she was going to need time to regain all her senses.

"If she moves ahead too quickly, it could have some adverse effects on her," Dr. Thor said as he prepared to leave. "Well, she's done it one more time hasn't she? She's proven to us once again what a strong willed person she really is hasn't she? Her will to live has beaten the odds once more."

"She sure has," Tom said smiling broadly.

"I'll look in on her in a week," Dr. Thor said. "If you feel the need for me to come sooner, just give me a call. Maybe after that, she can come see me instead of me coming to her," he added as he smiled and left.

Jason sat beside Andrea's bed as she rested. He found it hard to believe she was finally out of her coma and, at the same time, she told him she loved him. He thought about all the time they had wasted by not admitting their love for each other sooner.

News of Andrea's recovery traveled fast. Their phone started ringing and wasn't stopping as people called to convey how happy they were that Andrea was going to be all right. They said it truly was a Christmas miracle.

Jason was concerned that the constant ringing of the phone would disturb Andrea's sleep. She still needed plenty of rest. Jason rose, leaving her sleeping peacefully and headed towards the study. He knew he would find Tom there.

As Jason entered Tom looked up and said, "Come in and sit down," as he nodded towards the chair in front of his desk.

"What's on your mind?" he asked.

"A couple of things," Jason stated. He hesitated for a moment.

"First off, I know I didn't ask your permission to marry Andrea, so I guess that's partly why I'm here. I'd like to have your permission and blessing to marry your daughter," Jason stated.

Tom rose, walked around his desk and stood in front of Jason. After watching him carefully for a few minutes, he placed a hand on Jason's shoulder and said, "I've known for a long time that you were in love with Andrea. I've also known that she was in love with you. I just didn't know if the two of you were ever going to work things out. I'm glad you did. I'd be proud to offer you her hand in marriage," he stated as he grinned widely at Jason.

Jason rose and shook Tom's hand and said, "Thank you sir. I'll take the best care of her I possibly can. I'll do my best to make her happy."

"That's all I can ask for," Tom said. "Now what was the second thing you wanted to talk to me about?"

"When do you plan on telling her about Alex and what happened to her?" Jason asked.

"I'm not sure," Tom said pausing then walking back towards his chair. "I know I can't wait much longer. She's already been asking too many questions about bits and pieces of things she's remembering. I'm just afraid of what it might do to her when she hears the whole story," he continued. "Hopefully, we'll be able to wait a couple more days before we have to tell her. Every day she's a little stronger. The longer we can put it off the better. I just don't know how long I can forestall her questions."

"I'd like to be with her when you tell her," Jason said.

"That's fine. I had hoped you would. I think it should come from her mother and I with you only in the room. You can probably answer some of her questions better than we can about what happened with Alex. So when we're telling her, if we leave something out that you feel she needs to know, please go ahead. I don't want the entire family there. That might put too much pressure on her," he said as he leaned back in his chair.

"I agree," Jason said and then left.

The next morning as Marabel was taking Andrea's breakfast tray up to her room, she overhead Andrea asking Daniel what had happened to her the night of the Taylor's ball.

"I remember going there with Jason and leaving with Ted. After that everything is blank," Andrea said.

Marabel pushed open her door saying, "Good morning, dearie, time for your breakfast. Daniel, your breakfast is waiting for you downstairs. You'd better go down and eat it before it gets cold," she said as she nodded at him to leave.

"Sure thing," Daniel said. "See you later." He left, thanking Marabel to himself for saving him from having to answer Andrea's question.

Andrea didn't think anything of Marabel's barging in. She figured Marabel just didn't have a free hand available to knock with. Andrea sat back and slowly drank her breakfast.

"This stuff is really awful. When do I get to sink my teeth into some real food?" she asked.

"You've only got a couple of more days to go on liquids, then we can give you something with a little more substance to it," Marabel responded. "But don't go expecting T-bone steak right away," she added with a smile.

"Marabel, how long was I in a coma?" Andrea asked.

"Oh, let's see, about . . . well, around five months," Marabel stated.

"That long!" Andrea said. "What happened to me?" she asked.

Marabel sat there a minute thinking. "Drink your breakfast child and don't go asking so many questions."

"Come on, why won't anyone tell me what happened? Jason, mom, dad, Daniel, George, you . . . you all avoid answering my questions! Why? Why?" she yelled as she slammed her glass down on her tray.

"It's for your own good," Marabel said as she straightened Andrea's tray back up.

"How can it be for my own good when it upsets me so? All I do is feel more and more confused?" she stated.

"Now child, don't go getting yourself all worked up. That isn't going to do you any good," Marabel said.

"I just want to know what happened to me. Is that asking too much?" Andrea pleaded.

"No, no it isn't. But that's a matter you're going to have to take up with your father. He has forbidden any of us to tell you anything," Marabel said.

"Well then you just go tell him that I want to talk with him about this matter and I mean right now!" Andrea demanded.

Marabel collected the tray and moved towards the kitchen. As she entered she said, "Mr. and Mrs. Higgins, you'd best get upstairs to Andrea's room and calm her down. She demands to know what happened to her and she's not going to rest until she's told I'm afraid," she said as she sat the tray down on the counter.

Tom looked over at Shirley. "Guess we can't wait any longer."

"I suppose not," Shirley said quietly.

"At least we gained a couple of days for her to get her strength up. Are you sure you're ready?" Tom asked Shirley.

"I guess I have to be. I sure hope Andrea is," Shirley responded.

"Daniel, do you know where Jason is?" Tom asked.

"I think he's still at home," Daniel answered.

"Go get him for me. Tell him the time has come to explain everything to Andrea," Tom said.

Daniel headed for Jason's house as Shirley and Tom started up the stairs to Andrea's room. Just as Daniel reached Jason's porch, Jason came strolling out the door.

"Jason," Daniel said. "I'm glad I caught you. Dad sent me over to get you. He asked that you to go right up to Andrea's room. She's demanding to know what happened to her. Mom and dad are finally going to tell her."

"Thanks," Jason said as he ran to the main house. When he reached Andrea's bedroom, he knocked on the door and waited for a reply.

"Come in," Tom said.

As Jason entered, Tom, Shirley and Andrea were waiting for him. It was obvious by the way Andrea looked at him that she was quite upset.

"It's about time you got here," she snapped. "Now, if you don't mind, would someone please fill me in on just what happened to me?"

"Andrea, this is going to be very hard for you, as well as for your father and myself. Please be a little patient with us. We intend to be patient with you and answer all of your questions. We don't want to rush into what we are about to tell you either. If at any time you think you don't want to hear anymore or don't understand, please stop us. Okay?" Shirley asked looking directly at her. Andrea nodded her head in agreement.

"We also thought you'd want Jason with you as we explain everything to you. Jason will be able to answer some of the questions you may have that we can't," Shirley added.

Suddenly Andrea felt very insecure. She'd never seen her parents look so serious in her life. Instinctively, she reached out for Jason's hand. Everyone noticed the intense look on her face and her quick reflex to reach out for Jason.

"Here it goes . . ." Tom said as he began to explain "Alex Longred's gang kidnapped you and took you to his place by force the night of the Taylor's ball. Do you remember going to the Taylor's ball?" he asked her.

"Yes, I remember going with Jason, but I . . . I remember leaving with Ted and then . . . nothing," she said as she nervously looked at her dad and then at Jason.

"Andrea, I'm going to go back and start at the beginning, the very beginning. When you were little, about four years old, something very tragic happened to you." Tom continued "I don't know how else to tell you this . . . but your . . . mother and I are not . . . your biological parents. We adopted you when you were four years old. You see, your biological mother was my . . . my sister."

Andrea's face went white. She looked at her mother and the back to her father, or at least to the individuals she had always believed where her mother and father.

"But . . ." Andrea started to say as she gripped Jason's hand tighter, so tight you could see the whites of her knuckles.

"Wait Andrea," her father said. "Before you say anything, do you want me to continue?" he asked taking her by the shoulders and looking directly into her eyes.

Feeling panic and confusion, Andrea still wanted to hear more.

"Yes" she whispered. Tom let go of her.

"You see, when you were four years old, your mother and father, my sister and her husband, died in a fire," he said.

Andrea suddenly gasped. The faces she kept seeing flash in her head at times when she was near fire were they her mother and father? She wasn't sure she'd be able to take much more, but Tom continued on.

"You also have a brother . . . a twin brother. Alex Longred is your twin brother," he stated.

Andrea's mind was racing. Alex was her twin brother? "But, why . . . how . . .?" she asked Tom.

"Just take it easy and I'll continue slowly," Tom said as he looked over at Shirley who was now crying softly.

"You met Alex Longred while you were away at college. Yes, that's where this nightmare began for you. Do you remember him showing up at the Flower Shop to take you out?" he asked her.

"Yes. I remember all that. I remember trying to get out of going out with him, but it didn't work so I wound up at the drive-in with him. Jason came to my rescue" she said.

"That's correct," Tom said. "But apparently, Alex didn't like that so he decided to kidnap you. That's where the Taylor's ball comes into play," he added.

"You left the ball with Ted Jones. Apparently you got upset with Jason and decided to leave with Ted. He was supposed to take you directly home because you had said you weren't feeling well. But Ted seemed to have had other ideas. He took you out to Miller Hill and he tired to take advantage of you. You got mad at him, got out his car, and started walking home. Alex's gang found you walking along the road and took you back to Alex's place." Tom paused to see how Andrea was reacting to all of this.

Andrea was slowly starting to remember things, but she kept seeing the faces of her real mother and father and that confused her all the more.

"Anyway," Tom continued, "when you got there, they locked you up in the attic. We still don't know for sure what he planned to do with you other then eventually . . . kill you," he said.

Andrea gasped.

"Jason figured out that Alex had you at his place and he and your brothers went to rescue you. I stayed behind with your mother. Not that I didn't want to help rescue you, but there's more to this story. When you were up in the attic, some old memories started coming back to you,

138

causing you go into shock. You found a trunk with a doll in it. This doll," he said as he held up the doll.

As she reached out to take the scorched doll, she suddenly dropped it. It felt hot to her touch. Tom picked up the doll and handed it to her again. This time she gingerly took it in her arms. The memories were once again flooding back to her.

"You see, Alex was always intrigued by fire and, as best we can tell, he set his parent's, your parent's, bedroom on fire. Then he took you up to the attic and that's where the two of you . . . you and Alex, were discovered by the firemen. You were holding on to this doll, but as the firemen were carrying you out, you dropped it. It was put in the trunk you found. Your real parents never had a chance of making it out of their room. We don't think they ever woke up. It happened very early in the morning," Tom said. Then he said to Andrea "Are you okay?"

With tears streaming down her face, once again she shook her head yes.

"We adopted you and attempted to send Alex to England to live with his uncle Lance, but it backfired. Lance came to America to live on your parent's estate. He fixed it up and made a new life for himself here. We felt it was best to keep you and Alex apart so we swore never to let you know what had happened. When Jason found you in the attic, you were in shock then you went into a coma. You stayed that way for months, similar to what happened to you before. Both times your body tried to kill itself, but your will to live is so strong, you managed to beat it," Tom said.

He stopped and waited a long time before saying, "Andrea, we love you as our very own daughter. Those feelings have not and will not ever change. When you've had time to comprehend all of this and are feeling better, we can tell you more about your parents. I'll show you pictures of your mother and father. You know every time I look at you I see my sister over and over again."

Then he hugged her and nodded to Shirley and Jason, "I think we should leave her alone for a while," then he gestured to for them to leave.

"You do want some time alone don't you?" he asked.

"Yes," she nodded. "Jason . . . please stay with me for a few minutes."

"Sure," Jason said, taking both of her hands in his as her parents left the room. Jason let Andrea sit in silence for a while before saying "Are you going to be all right?"

"I think so," she said looking at him. "I'm just so confused. Everything dad said has slowly come back to me, but I don't understand why Alex wanted to kill me? Doesn't he know I'm his sister?"

"No, or at least he didn't know that when he kidnapped you. When he found you cradling the doll in the attic, Cindy and I told him that you were his twin sister, but he refused to believe it. I haven't gone to see him since they put him in jail. I doubt much has changed," Jason said.

"I think I'd like to be alone now. I just want to sort things out in my mind. I want to try to make some sense out of everything," she stated.

"Okay," Jason said. "But if you need anything, just yell."

"Okay," she said as she closed her eyes and rested her head on her pillow. Her mind was racing with everything she had just heard. She suddenly felt very weak and tired. Maybe if I can just get some rest, when I wake up, I'll be able to make some sense out of all of this, she thought and it wasn't long before she fell asleep.

Jason had gone to the door. As he was slowly closing the door he watched Andrea. She looked so weary. It was an awful lot for her to digest. He stood there a minute and realized she was already asleep. Good he thought.

Rest is what she needs and he closed the door the rest of the way.

Jason walked into the kitchen where he found Tom and Shirley sitting at the table. They both looked exhausted.

"I think she handled everything pretty well . . . all things considered that is," he said as he joined them.

Shirley poured him a cup of coffee and asked, "Do you think she's alright?"

"Yes. I think she just needs some time to herself and rest. Right now she's not sure who she is or just where she belongs," Jason said.

"She knows she belongs with us!" Shirley snapped.

"Yes, of course she does. But she's completely confused. Everything that is familiar to her has been turned upside down. I'm sure everything will work out. She needs time," Jason said. "When I left her room she, was sleeping. It wore her out physically as well as mentally. Sleep is the best thing for her right now."

"We need to keep a close watch on her right now. If she shows any signs of a relapse, we need to get Dr. Thor here immediately," Tom said.

Chapter Nine

Andrea was recovering quicker than anyone thought possible. On Dr. Thor's next visit, she asked him if it would be all right for her to have tutor come to the house and tutor her on the subjects she needed to complete for her degree requirements. She wanted to be able to graduate in the spring. Dr. Thor thought it would be fine, as long as she didn't over do it. So Andrea forged ahead with her subjects slowly and carefully.

She had already managed to walk on her own down the stairs and her and Jason began taking short walks together each afternoon when the weather permitted. When the weather was too cold for a walk, Jason would take her for short drives in his car.

The next afternoon, Jason arrived as usual for their afternoon walk.

"Let's take a drive instead of going for walk today. Okay?" he asked Andrea.

"The weather is really nice today. The snow should look especially pretty today since the sun is shining on it. Why don't you want to go for a walk?" she asked.

"No particular reason. I just feel like driving instead of walking today. But take your scarf and mittens just in case we do decide to stop and walk around," he added.

"Okay, if that's what you want," Andrea said as she grabbed her winter coat.

"Ready?" he asked.

Nodding yes they walked out and got in his car.

Jason was going to surprise her by taking her to a special spot where they could see for miles just how beautiful the sun glistening on the snow was.

Andrea was looking out the window. Snow had fallen the night before and was hanging on the trees making them glisten. She wasn't really paying attention to where they were heading.

As Jason turned into the entrance to Sugar Loaf Mountain, Andrea looked over at him quizzically. "What are we doing here?" she asked. "I can't go skiing."

"I know, but I've arranged it with the owner for us to ride the ski lift up to the top of the mountain so we can enjoy the view. He also helped me arrange to have a snowmobile waiting for us to use to come back down the mountain," Jason said smiling at her.

"Oh Jason it's wonderful!" she said as she leaned over and kissed him.

Getting out of the car, they headed to the lifts. The mountain had very few people skiing on it. Andrea felt it was a shame that more people weren't out enjoying the sun and the slopes.

Jason had also asked the ski lift operator if he would be able to stop the lift as they got to the top. He knew Andrea wouldn't be able to hop off the lift like the skiers do. He said they'd be happy to accommodate him. As they arrived at the top, just as the operator said, he stopped the ski lift and Jason gently helped Andrea off.

"Jason," Andrea said, "It's breathtaking. You can see so far today. The sky is so clear and blue."

Hand in hand, they strolled about the mountaintop taking it all in.

"Look at Lake Michigan," Andrea said at she pointed at it "it's turquoise color shows through so brilliantly where the ice is thin. This is wonderful. No matter which way you look, the scene is truly magnificent."

Andrea stopped to take in the sites and sounds of it all "I can't help but marvel at God's creation. I never get tired of seeing it. Don't you think it's beautiful?" she asked.

Jason didn't answer. He was watching her. Her eyes gleamed with excitement. She looked lovely. Reaching for her, he pulled her close to him. Smelling her soft scented perfume, he gazed into her eyes and kissed her.

He kissed her with such passion she felt her body begin to tingle all over. She kissed him back with the same intensity. She finally managed to pull herself away.

Jason felt her shiver and thought she was getting cold. "Let's go over to the warming shack," and taking her hand he led her towards it.

When they got to the door of the warming shack, Jason stopped and said to Andrea, "Now you need to close your eyes."

"Why?" she asked.

"Just trust me, please," he said.

"All right" she stated.

Jason led her inside.

"Okay now open your eyes," he said.

As Andrea opened her eyes, she was thrilled at what she saw. The warming shack had been transformed into a beautiful dining room. A table had been set with a white lace tablecloth, candles and dinner for the two of them. It made the room look cozy and warm. Soft music was playing in the background. The warming shack had windows on all four sides and with the sun shining in, it made the room even warmer.

"What's all this?" she asked.

Jason looked so happy. "I wanted to make this day special for you."

"What's the occasion?" she asked.

"Let's just wait and see what happens," he said. "Here, let me help you take your coat off," he took her coat off, placed it on a chair and did the same with his. Walking over to the table he said, "Please sit down."

Andrea walked over to the chair and as she sat down, Jason gently pushed the chair in for her and walked around to his chair to sit down.

"Care for something to drink?" he asked as he held up a chilled bottle of non-alcohol champagne.

"Certainly," she said and he poured them each a glass.

Jason opened up the two trays setting in front of them. Inside was a wonderful hot meal of stuffed chicken breasts, steamed broccoli, dinner rolls and for dessert Andrea's favorite, a homemade raspberry pie.

Making small talk as they ate, Andrea noticed that Jason was acting nervous and she didn't know why.

After they had finished their desert, Jason stood up and walked over to Andrea and he got down on one knee.

Andrea sat smiling at him.

"Andrea," Jason said quietly. "I know you already said you'd marry me but the way I asked you to marry me wasn't the way I had dreamed of asking you, so . . ." he said taking a ring out of his pocket and holding it out for her to see, "will you marry me?"

"Oh Jason, of course I will," she said as her eyes shined with tears.

Jason placed the ring on her finger. It was beautiful and gleamed in the sunlight, just like the snow.

They both stood up and she put her arms around him pulling him as close to her as possible. Then they kissed a long, passionate kiss. They stood staring into each other's eyes.

Jason finally broke the silence. "You know we haven't talked about a date for our wedding. I was thinking maybe the sooner the better." He wasn't sure how long he could keep from forcing himself on her and he wanted their first moments together to be perfect. He knew she wouldn't give herself completely to him unless she was his wife and he really didn't want it to be any other way.

"I've been waiting for you to bring up that subject," Andrea said. "I've always dreamed of a June wedding. How about June 18th?" She asked, staring up at him with a big beautiful smile on her face.

"Okay," he said and kissed her again. "I didn't want to wait that long but if you've always wanted a June wedding, then June it is."

Andrea wanted to stay on top of the mountain until the sunset, but Jason reminded her that she still needed to take it easy, so they bundled up and headed to the waiting snowmobile for the ride down the mountain.

As they got to Jason's car, Andrea said, "Jason, thank you so much for today. It couldn't have been more perfect." She leaned over and kissed him.

"I'm glad you enjoyed it," he said. "Now let's get you back so you can rest." They drove straight back to Andrea's house.

Andrea jumped out of the car and ran into the house. She didn't wait for Jason.

"Hey" Jason yelled. "Take it easy. You're not supposed to run!" But it was no use. She was already in the door.

"Hello! Where is everybody?" she yelled.

"In here," Tom called from the living room where the rest of the family sat. They were waiting for them to come back as they all knew what Jason had planned.

"Guess what?" Andrea sang happily as she walked in the room and sat down. Jason walked in the room a minute later.

"What?" her mother asked as if she couldn't guess.

"Jason officially asked me to marry him today. Look!" she said as she held out her hand with the ring on it.

"It's beautiful!" Shirley exclaimed.

George whistled. "That must have cost you a pretty penny," he said looking at Jason.

"We've also set a date. We're going to be married on June 18th" Andrea sang out joyously.

"What?" her mother said. "That's only a few months away. That doesn't give me enough time to put together a wedding. I'll never be able to manage in time," Shirley continued almost in a panic.

"But mom," Andrea said, "I've always wanted a June wedding."

"And we don't want to wait any longer. I've wasted too much time already without her," Jason said.

"Well, all right," Shirley relented. "But we've got to get started right away making arrangements."

"Dad," Andrea said as she turned towards her father and drastically changed the conversation. "Do you know when Alex's trial is going to be?"

This was the first time she had mentioned Alex's name since they had told her he was her twin brother.

After pausing for quite some time, Jason answered her question for her father, "In two weeks."

Tom hadn't wanted to answer his daughter. He had hoped to keep her from hearing anything about the trial until right before it was to begin. He wanted her strength to be built up as much as possible before she had to deal with testifying at her own twin brother's trial. Now he knew there was no way of keeping it from her.

"Good. I want to be there for the whole trial," Andrea stated.

"Do you think that's wise?" Shirley asked her.

"Why not?" Andrea replied.

"Are you sure you want to go through all that?" Shirley asked.

"Well, after all, he is my brother," Andrea stated.

"Jason, will you take me to see him tomorrow?" Andrea asked.

Jason looked over at Tom and Tom nodded in agreement.

"I guess so," he said.

Tom sat still for a few minutes thinking about the consequences of Andrea going to the jail and facing Alex for the first time since everything happened. He didn't want her to go, but he also knew he couldn't stop her.

"I guess I can't keep you from him forever. You are a big girl and I have to respect your decisions. Go ahead and see him, but please use extreme caution. Don't let yourself in for anymore then you think you'll be able to handle," Tom sighed quietly.

The next morning, Jason drove Andrea to the county jail.

"Andrea," Jason said before he opened the door, "are you really sure about this?"

"Yes I am," she stated.

"Okay," he said. "But you know it's not too late to turn around and go back home."

"Look, he's my brother and I have to go see him. Can't anyone understand that? I've fought with this inside me for the past few weeks. I have to go see him before his trial starts. I just have to," she stated as she got out of Jason's car.

"I just want you to understand that you might not be able to deal with what you're about to see," Jason said. "Or if Alex will see you."

"That's something I'll just have to find out for myself," Andrea said flatly.

They entered the county jail. Andrea asked the clerk if it would be possible for her to see Alex Longred. He stated she could, but that it was necessary to have bars separating them. He indicated that Alex's mental state had worsened and he was becoming quite violent. The clerk then left to set things up for their meeting. When he returned he motioned for Andrea to follow him.

"I'm coming too," Jason said.

Andrea stopped in her tracks. "No," she snapped. "I want to see him alone."

"I'm not letting you go in there by yourself," Jason replied.

"Oh yes you are Jason and that's final!" she stated.

Jason looked surprised at her forceful response and at the tone of voice she had used. Jason wanted to go in with her, but after that response he knew better than to argue with her.

"It's just that I feel strongly about seeing my twin brother alone, that's all," she said as she placed a hand on his arm.

"Oh, all right," he said with much reluctance.

Andrea quickly followed the clerk. He led her down a narrow corridor and into a small room with bars down the center. He showed her where to sit and then left. She didn't have to wait long before a guard entered with Alex following close behind in chains.

"I couldn't believe my ears when the guard told me that the all high and mighty Andrea Higgins had come to see me," Alex said as he sat down across from her. His chains rattled loudly in the small room.

"Just what do you want with me?" he continued. "Do you want to gloat over the fact that I'm finally behind bars?"

"No, that's not it at all," Andrea said. She began slowly. "Has anyone explained to you what the relationship between us is?"

"Relationship between us . . . what the hell are you talking about?" he asked.

"No one has told you that . . . that you are my twin brother?" she asked.

"You've got to be kidding! We're not related in any way!" he yelled.

"Oh yes we are!" Andrea yelled back.

"Like hell . . . the last thing I want in this world is to be related to you! The only relationship between us is the one where I almost killed you, and believe me, if I ever get out of here, that's exactly what I'm going to do. I'm going to kill you! Guard, let me out of here," he demanded as he stood up knocking his chair over. The guard let Alex out and took him back to his cell.

Why is he so violent towards me? Why can't he understand that we're brother and sister? Andrea was thoroughly confused. Tears ran down her face. Sitting quietly for a few moments she composed herself and headed back to Jason. It hadn't gone at all like she had hoped or planned. She'd hoped to explain everything to him and tell him that no matter what it took, she would see to it that he got the help he needed. She just couldn't understand him. Maybe I never will, she thought.

Jason rose as she entered the room. He could tell she'd been crying. "How did it go?" he asked.

"Oh Jason," she said running to him, placing her arms around him. "He doesn't want to be my brother. He just wants to kill me," she said as she began to cry once again.

"It's all right, honey," Jason said as he pulled her closer to him. "He needs help. He can't help the way he acts."

"I know, I know," Andrea said and turned to ask the clerk, "When is Alex's trial going to begin?"

The clerk looked through his papers and said, "Here it is . . . his bench trial is at nine o'clock a week from this Monday morning in Courtroom C. Judge Brown will be hearing the case."

"Thank you." Turning to Jason, Andrea asked, "Does he have an attorney?"

"Of course he does," Jason said half smiling. "His uncle Lance . . . your uncle Lance is an attorney, remember?"

"Yes, of course, my uncle Lance. I just forgot for a moment," she said.

"Let's go home now," he said. They headed for his car then drove home.

Tom was waiting for Andrea. He went to the door when he heard Jason's car pull up.

"How did it go?" he asked Andrea as she got out of the car and headed for the house.

Before Andrea could answer, Jason said, "Not well. Andrea had quite a time with him. Let's just let her relax now, okay?"

Tom nodded. He understood exactly what Jason had meant. Jason felt she might not be able to deal with anything more right now, especially talking to her father about Alex.

"Yes," Andrea said, "I'd like to go upstairs and rest now." She headed towards the stairs, but before she got there, she stopped and asked her father "Would you speak to uncle Lance and make sure he's doing everything in his power to make sure Alex gets everything he needs?"

"Sure" her dad said.

When Andrea was out of sight and Jason was sure she wouldn't be able to hear them talking, he informed Tom of what had taken place.

Chapter Ten

Alex's trial was about to begin. Andrea said she would be attending his trial everyday until it was finished. She wanted to be sure everything turned out as she hoped it would. When Andrea informed Jason of her intentions, he told her she'd have to go by herself. He didn't think he could stand being in the same room with Alex for that long and maintain control over his hatred for him. Jason indicated to Andrea that the only time he would be in the courtroom was when he had to testify. Andrea was still determined to go and remain there with her brother until the very end.

Jason didn't like this, but he understood. Also, he was kind of proud of her devotion and determination to help her brother out.

As Andrea sat in the courtroom listening to testimony after testimony, she prayed the judge would come to the conclusion that Alex should be in a mental institution for the criminally insane. It was obvious from everyone's testimony that was where he belonged. Jason had been true to his word. He appeared in the courtroom, only during the time he had to testify.

When it came time for her to testify, she nervously approached the stand. As she sat down in the chair, she looked over at Alex who was staring straight into her eyes. Her blood ran cold. He really did want to kill her . . . she could see the hatred in his eyes. Even so, as she testified, she continued to add wherever possible that Alex definitely did not have control over his own emotions, and what he needed was help. She stated several times that Alex acted as if other forces were running his life. She knew the judge listened to her . . . she just hoped she had said enough to help.

After her testimony was finished, which took the better part of two days, the judge rose to go to his chambers to make his decision. Andrea sat staring at Alex who was obviously avoiding looking at her now. She wanted him to know that she was concerned and cared about what happened to him even if he did hate her. When she was on the stand, she stared at him for quite some time and she still found it hard to believe he was her twin brother, but deep inside she felt it and knew it was true. Someday, maybe Alex would feel it too.

After about three and a half hours, Judge Brown returned to the courtroom. He sat down and began to state his findings.

"After carefully weighing all the facts in this case, I have no other choice but to place Alex Longred in the Thread Hurst Mental Institution for the criminally insane for the rest of his natural life," the Judge said as he slammed his gavel down. "Court dismissed."

Andrea gave a long sigh of relief. At least he won't be in a jail cell for the rest of his life, she thought. Rising slowly she started walking towards where Alex sat hanging his head.

The two officers who were assigned to Alex noticed Andrea approaching. As she neared him, they each took a hold of Alex's arms to restrain him. They didn't want Alex to be able to touch Andrea for fear of what he might do to her.

Andrea looked directly at Alex and said, "Alex, even though we've been through some pretty tough times together, and even though you hate me, you're still my twin brother. That's a fact that I'll never deny. Please take care of yourself."

Alex looked at her and she thought she saw his eyes softening, when he said, "The evidence may have proved that you're my biological sister but for all I care . . ." then he hung his head as the officers took him away.

Andrea sat down and started crying. Jason came up behind her and placed his hands on her shoulders. She hadn't realized he had been in the courtroom that day, but she knew it was his touch without even looking. She finally did look up at him and rose to have him hold her as she continued to cry. Jason understood. After all, twins have a common bond between them that no one else but another twin can understand or feel. Part of her was breaking in two. Part of her was going into a mental institution for the rest of his life. She was having trouble dealing with it. Jason placed an arm around her waist and helped her walk out of the courtroom.

Andrea suddenly stopped crying. She swore to herself that she could hear her real mother's voice saying, "It'll be all right Andrea. Please don't worry. Alex is going to get the care and treatment he needs. We don't have to worry about him anymore." She composed herself right then and there and from that day on she told herself, she wouldn't shed another tear over her twin brother.

Chapter Eleven

With Alex's trial finished the Higgins household became a beehive of activity planning Andrea and Jason's wedding. Andrea was having weekly fittings for her wedding gown that Marabel was designing. In between times, she had gone to the college to fill out the necessary forms to receive her college degree. Dr. Thor had thought it best if she didn't participate in the graduation ceremony with all the excitement going on surrounding her upcoming nuptials. She consented to having her degree mailed to her and concentrated on her wedding.

She and Jason had to drive all over town making arrangements for their wedding. Everything was so exciting to Andrea. She was finally going to marry the one true love of her life. The two of them were so busy they hardly had any time to be by themselves.

As their wedding day approached all the necessary final arrangements were being made for it to be held on the garden patio. The reception was going to be held under a tent next to the cherry orchards. There were going to be about 1,000 guests in attendance. This wedding was going to be the social event of the year.

Andrea awoke early on the day of her wedding. She couldn't sleep and there was plenty for her to do before two o'clock came around. She heard noises from downstairs as people began getting up and moving about. Many of her out of town guests had arrived the night before and were staying at Cherry Wood Manor. Dressing quickly, she ran down the stairs.

Poking her head into the kitchen first, she wanted to be sure Jason wasn't sitting at the kitchen table. He wasn't, so she went on in. She didn't want to jinx their new life together by seeing him before the wedding. It wasn't proper for the groom to see his bride before the wedding ceremony on their wedding day. Tom and Shirley were sitting in the kitchen. Their guests were being served in the main dining room. But they wanted some time to themselves before the day's activities began. They had a few details to be discussed yet.

"Good morning," Andrea said cheerfully.

"You're up early," Shirley said. "I figured you'd want to sleep late today."

"No, I couldn't," Andrea said. "I'm so excited I couldn't sleep and besides, I have a few things I have to do today before I get married."

"I see," her mother said. "Like what?"

"Oh just a couple of things," Andrea stated. "First, I want a light breakfast. Marabel, some tea and toast, please."

"Don't you think you should eat more than that?" Marabel asked.

"No, I don't think I could keep much more down anyway. My stomach is full of butterflies," she said quickly as she ate the toast Marabel had sat down in front of her.

"Dad, may I borrow your car for a while please?" she asked.

"I guess so," he said. "But where are you going?"

"Just out to run errand," she said.

"Andrea, this is your wedding day. Don't go taking off too far," he added.

"Now dad, really," she said with a big smile on her face. "Do you think I'd be late for my own wedding?"

"No," he said. "But then again, I never know what trouble you might get into. Do you really have to go someplace?"

"Yes dad," she said. "What I have to do must be done today," and with that she took his keys and headed out the door.

"That's strange," Shirley said. "I wonder what she has to do before she gets married?"

With puzzled looks on their faces, they watched her drive away.

Jason rose early too. He decided to stay inside his house. He didn't think he should intrude on the Higgins family breakfast on such an important day. He felt it was important that the family have breakfast with Andrea today without his presence. He also knew how old-fashioned Andrea was with regard to traditions. She had said to him last night that at the stroke of twelve he was to go home and not try to see her until she was walking down the aisle towards him. Is it really going to come true? Is she really going to become my wife?

Turning to look out his window he saw her coming out the back door and getting into her dad's car. Where on earth was she going? And today of all days! Everything she could possibly need is in that house already. She didn't have to go anywhere. Even her hairdresser is coming to the house to do her hair. Where is she going? What is she going to do? Jason was confused.

Andrea knew in her heart she had to do this. Her wedding day wouldn't be complete without it. It had taken her a long time to build up enough courage, but it had to be today or never. She drove the car out of town. After driving for about an hour and 15 minutes, she turned off the road and into a little cemetery. It hadn't been easy to find out where her parents had been laid to rest. Her adopted father really covered his tracks well in hiding their graves. It had all been done out of love and for her own good. She understood that. She stopped the car, turned off the ignition and sat trying to get control of herself. After a few minutes, she got out of the car and started reading headstones. Quite some time later, she found the ones she had been searching for.

157

"Sandra and Harry Longred . . . May they rest in Peace and God be with them always," she read aloud. Then she knelt as she touched their headstone.

"Mom, dad," she choked on the words, "it's me, your daughter, Andrea. I bet you never thought I would come here. I know it's been a long time since you heard from me, but I realize you know all about that. I came to tell you how sorry I am about what happened . . . you know Alex was ill . . . he still is. I'm sure in his own way, he loved you very much. He just didn't know how to handle what was happening to him. He was too young to know what was going on. Anyway, he's being taken care of now. And me . . . well I'm about to marry the most wonderful man in the whole wide world. He's . . . well . . . I'm sure you know more about what's happening then I do, but mom . . . dad, I came here today to . . . to get some sign of approval from you. A sign that you agree with my choice of a husband. I know that sounds absurd, but I wouldn't marry him if you didn't approve of him. I have to know . . ." and she waited in silence as the minutes passed. Then a gentle breeze came up and she thought she could hear her mother and father saying together, "Yes, Andrea, he's a wonderful man. He is the right one for you."

Andrea smiled inside. "Thank you Lord, thank you for letting mom and dad reach out to me today and for leading me to them." She blew a kiss towards her parents' names on the headstone. She knew in her heart they understood. Rising quickly, she hurried to her car. She still had things to do when she reached home. She had already been gone longer then she had planned.

Returning to her bedroom, she found Marabel anxiously waiting for her with the hairdresser. "It's about time you returned young lady," she snapped, "We're certainly going to be rushed for time now," as she grabbed Andrea and whirled her into the bathroom so the hairdresser could begin.

As Marabel was adding the finishing touches to her wedding dress, she looked at Andrea and noticed that she had a radiant glow about her that she hadn't had before she left the house that morning. Marabel wondered why.

When the hairdresser finished with her hair, Andrea walked over to the window where she could see the garden patio being transformed into a wedding chapel. Is this a dream? Am I really getting married? She felt so happy.

Tom was ready and walked over to where Jason was waiting and found him nervously pacing up and down.

"Jason, calm down," Tom said. "You look as though you're having second thoughts."

"No, sir," Jason stated. "It's just that . . . well is Andrea back yet?"

"Andrea? You saw her leave this morning did you?" Tom asked. And then added, "Yes, she's back. She's been back for about an hour and half. Really, Jason, you're usually more observant," Tom said as he smiled at Jason.

"Do you know where she went?" Jason asked.

"No," Tom said. "I don't. The whole thing is a little strange. She said it was something she had to do today. I was hoping you knew what it was."

"I haven't any idea," Jason said. "She never said anything to me. As a matter of fact, just last night she said she was sure everything had been taken care of because she had gone over the list three times herself."

"Well, whatever it was," Tom said, "she's here now and that's what counts."

Jason nodded in agreement, but he intended to find out just what was so important that it had to be done on the morning of their wedding.

While Shirley was tending to their guests and the last minute preparations on the patio, Marabel was helping

Andrea get into her wedding dress when Tom knocked on the door. "Andrea, may I come in?" he asked.

"Yes dad," she replied.

What Tom saw as he opened the bedroom door made him gasp out loud. He was seeing his sister on her wedding day.

"What's the matter daddy?" Andrea asked.

"Nothing sweetheart," he said shaking his head. "It's just that . . . that . . . "

Andrea interrupted him, "I remind you of Sandra, don't' I?" she said.

He nodded yes.

"It's all right dad," she said. "I understand."

"You look lovely," he finally said.

"Thank you dad," she said. They stood looking at each other for a few moments.

"Well, this is the big day," he said. "Any questions?"

"No dad," Andrea smiled. "Mom had that talk with me a long time ago."

"Well, after all," he said. "I'm losing my little girl." He paused . . . "I'm only trying to do what Sandra and Harry would have wanted me to do."

"Dad," Andrea said walking over to him, "there's something I want to tell you. I love you and mom dearly and I always will. You have treated me as your very own child, and I'm not so sure how I would have turned out if you hadn't . . . maybe I would have been like Alex. I don't know. But this morning . . . I . . . I went to find my parents' graves. I know that sounds like a funny thing to do on your wedding day, but I felt I just had to. I felt I had to have their permission to marry Jason. Do you understand that?" she asked him.

"Yes, I believe I do," he said. "And did you get their approval?"

"Believe it or not, dad, I thought I actually heard them say, yes. At least in my heart I did," she said.

Tom hugged his daughter. "Good, I'm glad you did that. Now we both know they approve and that all is well," he added as he kissed her on her cheek.

"How did you find their graves?" he asked.

"It wasn't easy. You sure did a good job of hiding them. I did a little investigating on my own and eventually found them," she said.

"Well, I'm glad you did, but you know you could have come to me and asked me where they were buried. I would have taken you there," he added.

"I know that now, but I didn't want to hurt you and mom by asking you to take me there so that I could talk with them. You do understand don't you?" she asked.

"Certainly," Tom said.

Tom hugged his daughter again as the wedding music began downstairs.

"I think that's our cue. Shall we go?" he asked gesturing for her to take his arm. She smiled as she placed her arm in his. She didn't need to answer. He could see the sparkle in her eyes and he knew she was ready.

He led her downstairs and to the patio doors where they waited for Shirley to join them. Even though Andrea was a strong believer in tradition, she wanted both her mother and her father to walk her down the aisle. As they waited for their cue to walk down the aisle, Andrea whispered "Mom, Dad, I love you."

"We love you too," they whispered back.

Everyone rose as they walked out onto the patio. Andrea made a truly beautiful bride. Marabel had done a marvelous job on her wedding dress. She made a tiara crown with a full-length veil to cover Andrea's face. The dress was cut low and very form fitting with a sheer taffeta overlay coming up to her neck meeting a Victorian lace collar. The dress flowed freely out from her waist with a ten-foot long train flowing behind her.

Walking beside her mother and father, she began to shake. She still wasn't able to see Jason and she found it hard to believe that this was truly happening. After a few more steps, she saw Jason's face as he stood there so magnificently in his tuxedo. He smiled brightly as he saw her and as their eyes met, her heart began to soar. It's true, she thought.

Jason could hardly believe his eyes. He knew she was beautiful but never in his wildest dreams could he perceive her looking even more beautiful, but once again she proved to him that she could. His hands became sweaty as she came closer to him.

The minister asked, "Who gives this bride?" Shirley and Tom responded, "We do."

Jason could hardly control himself as he took Andrea's hand in his. He felt a warming sensation throughout his body as she looked at him through her veil.

"Ladies and Gentlemen, we have gathered here today to join this man and this woman in holy matrimony. Andrea and Jason have composed their own vows and now they will commit the rest of their lives to each other before God and all of you as their witnesses," the minister stated as he stepped back to let Jason and Andrea begin with their vows.

Jason turned and looked into Andrea's eyes. Then he took her hands in his and began. "Andrea, I love you with all my heart. From this day forward I pledge to you my body and soul. They are yours to keep for eternity. Let all of Heaven ring out in joyous revelation as I pledge my love to you. When our earthly lives have come to an end, may God see it fit for us to continue our love in the hereafter," and he took her ring and placed it upon her finger.

"Please take this ring as an outward sign of my undying love and devotion solely to you," he said.

Andrea could hardly believe the beautiful words she had just heard. Did Jason really love her that much? Now it was her turn.

"Jason, I too love you with all of my heart and pledge to you my body and soul now and through eternity. Our love has withstood many separations in the past, may the future only bring us closer together forever," she said as she took his ring and placed it upon his finger.

"Please take this ring as a sign of my undying love and devotion to you. I will cherish you for all our lives. I will follow you wheresoever the future leads. I am willfully becoming your wife, your companion and your sole mate. I will love you always and forever until there is no tomorrow. For when there is no tomorrow, no life will exist anywhere not even in the Heavens," and she looked deeply into his eyes.

The minister then stated, "You may kiss the bride."

Jason slowly lifted her veil with trembling hands, pulled her close and kissed her with such passion and feeling that the minister had to nudge them to stop.

"Ladies and Gentlemen, may I present to you, Mr. and Mrs. Jason Steele" he announced.

As Andrea and Jason turned to face the gathering, they smiled warmly at each other then quickly headed towards the cherry grove where the reception was to be held. Standing in the reception line at the entrance to the tent and greeting their many guests, they began to wonder if the line would ever end. As soon as the line ended, Jason said to Andrea "Follow me." They both laughed at running away from their own reception for a few minutes. Jason was leading her into the cherry grove.

"Finally," Jason said, "a few moments alone with you."

"Yes," she said as she let him put his arms around her.

"Well Mrs. Steele," Jason said, "are you as happy as I am?"

163

"Of course, I am," she answered and they embraced in a long and passionate kiss.

Jason couldn't wait to make her solely his. He pressed himself against her even harder . . . harder . . . and then they heard her mother calling them.

"Andrea! Jason! Really now, just where did those two run off too? After all, they have guests to attend to," she was saying to Tom.

"Now Shirley," Tom replied, as he pointed to Andrea and Jason who were slowly emerging from the cherry grove, "I think they just wanted a few seconds alone."

"Really," Shirley huffed as they walked over to Andrea and Jason and pulled a twig out of Andrea's veil.

"Do you think you two can control yourselves for a just a little longer and visit with your guests?" she snapped.

Andrea just blushed as she and Jason headed back towards their awaiting guests.

As they entered the tent and headed towards the wedding party table, their guests broke out in applause. Andrea and Jason sat down so the minister could say grace and dinner could be served. As the minister finished saying grace the caterers began bringing out the first course of their meal. Andrea and Jason chatted with everyone in their wedding party during their meal. As dinner was finished they cut the cake and, once again, they broke with tradition. To everyone's amazement Jason and Andrea personally served the cake to all their quests.

Once they had finished serving the cake, the band began to play. From that moment on Jason was only able to get a few seconds with Andrea before someone else was off dancing with her. Jason was in demand by all of their female guests as well. They danced until well into the evening.

Finally the time arrived for the bride and groom to say their goodbyes.

As they prepared to leave, all the single girls in attendance gathered near Andrea in hopes of catching her bouquet. Who happened to catch it? Cindy.

"Well," Andrea said smiling at Jason, "maybe she will be next. At least that's all she got from me . . . my flowers and not you." Then she laughed out loud.

Then all the single men gathered near Jason as he removed the garter belt from Andrea's leg and threw it to them. Daniel was the lucky one to catch it.

Jason walked over to Daniel and slapped him on the back saying "So, is there someone you haven't told us about? Have you been seeing someone secretly? Are you going to be next?"

Daniel blushed and said, "I don't think I'm ready to settle down. Besides I haven't found the right girl yet."

Andrea and Jason waved goodbye to their guests. Then they turned to her mother and father. Andrea hugged her mother and father kissing them the cheek. Jason shook Tom's hand and then he hugged Shirely.

"Thank you mom and dad for everything you've done for us," Andrea said with tears in her eyes.

"Yes, thank you," Jason added.

"You're welcome," Tom said. "We have one last surprise for the two of you."

"What's that?" Andrea asked.

Tom looked towards the central cherry barn and nodded his head. They heard a loud sound and then the sky lit up with fireworks spreading across the sky. The fireworks lasted for quite a few minutes. Andrea had tears streaming down her face as she watched the grand finale of the fireworks.

"Mom, dad," Andrea said. "I don't know what to say. They were fantastic just like both of you."

"You don't need to say anything dear," Shirley said. "Now the two of you get out of hear. Your honeymoon awaits."

They hugged each other again and then they left.

Settling into the car, Andrea asked, "I know you wanted to keep our honeymoon a big secret, even from me, but don't you think now, since we're about to be on our way, you could bring yourself to tell me just where it is that we will be going?"

"Nope," Jason said, "not yet." Then they pulled out of the driveway and began driving around town for what seemed like a couple of hours then Jason turned down a little dirt path that Andrea knew only led back to her house, but from the backside of the orchard. No one used this road anymore. It had grown up with weeds. She asked Jason, "What are you doing? Did you forget something? This only goes back to my house?"

"I know. We're going to spend our honeymoon in the cottage house. Our new home from now on. I know that doesn't sound like much of a place to honeymoon . . . but I wanted our first night together to be perfect. I couldn't think of a more perfect spot then where we would be spending the rest of our lives together. Do you mind?" he asked her.

"Oh, Jason," she said. "I think that's about the sweetest thing I've ever heard."

Jason pulled the car off into a grove of cherry trees where he was sure no one would be able to see it, and together they crept up to the house, being very careful so that any remaining guests wouldn't see them. As they got to the front door, Jason picked her up in his arms and carried her over the threshold and into their bedroom. He kissed her again before placing her feet upon the floor. Carefully he pulled the curtains closed, lit a candle beside the bed and put soft music on. The two of them stood looking at each other.

She nervously looked around the room then said, "Give me a couple of minutes to change." She headed for the bathroom taking her night case with her.

Jason quickly undressed, climbed into bed and poured two glasses of champagne.

Andrea stood in the bathroom feeling very nervous. Why am I so nervous? I love Jason and this is what I've dreamed of so many times. I've got to get control of myself, she thought. Turning off the light she slowly opened the door.

There in the candlelight, Jason was able to see the outline of her body beneath her negligee. His eyes slowly wandered the full length of her body. She was so beautiful and now . . . now she was all his. He finally spoke.

"You're beautiful sweetheart. Please come sit here beside me," he said as he patted the bed.

Andrea moved gracefully to him. She was surprised at how poised she was as she sat down beside him.

"Here," he said as he handed her a glass of champagne. "Let's toast to our future. To us, Mr. and Mrs. Jason Steele. May we always be as happy as we are tonight."

They each took a sip and then set their glasses down and melted into each other's arms. They drifted off into a night of sweet ecstasy.

Chapter Twelve

Andrea and Jason spent a quiet week alone in the cottage house. It took about two days before anyone from the Higgins household realized they were there, but they left them alone. They knew that Andrea and Jason wanted it that way.

Andrea and Jason adjusted quickly to married life. As each day passed, they felt their love continuing to grow.

Andrea found it exceptionally easy to settle herself into Jason's house. She was even learning to become quite a good cook. She hadn't done much cooking, as Marabel had always done the cooking for her family. She was taking lessons from her and learning quickly. Jason told Andrea it would be all right if they ate their meals with her family, but she didn't want it that way.

Jason and Andrea had hopes of starting a family right away and it wasn't long before it happened.

One morning, as Andrea rose early to get Jason's breakfast ready before he went to work, she became sick to her stomach while fixing eggs. She ran into the bathroom and threw up. Jason had only stirred a little, so she didn't think he heard her and she didn't want to bother him, so she went back to fixing his breakfast. When she had breakfast about ready, she woke him. They ate a leisurely breakfast together and then Jason headed out the door to start his day. Andrea quickly went to the phone and called Dr. Thor.

"Dr. Thor, this is Andrea Higgins, I mean Andrea Steele. Would it be possible for you to see me sometime this morning?" she asked.

"I can work you in Andrea, but what seems to be the trouble?" he asked.

"No trouble really, it's just that . . . well . . . I'd rather wait and tell you when I get there," he said.

"Andrea, what seems to be the problem? I need to know so I can determine how quickly I need to work you in," the doctor added.

"Well, doctor, I think I might be pregnant," she said.

"I want to see you immediately," he said. "You come right over. I'll have my nurse take you directly back to an examination room. I'll be waiting for you," and then he hung up. He was very concerned about her health if indeed she was pregnant. She had been through too much in the last year to let a pregnancy go on for very long without constant care and observation. He hoped everything would be all right.

Andrea hung up wondering why he wanted to see her immediately, but she showered, dressed and wrote a note for Jason that she had to run some errands and would be back later. She left for Dr. Thor's office.

As she entered his office, the nurse nodded to Andrea to follow her and took her directly back to where Dr. Thor was waiting for her.

Dr. Thor left her room after examining her. Returning to her room he said, "Congratulations are in order Andrea. You definitely are going to be a mother."

"Oh thank you Dr. Thor," Andrea said delighted. "I can't wait to tell Jason."

"Now, there are a few things you're going to have to be very careful about in regards to this pregnancy," Dr. Thor continued.

"Why so much concern doctor? Is something wrong?" Andrea asked.

"No, nothing is wrong. It's just that your body has been through so much within this last year, that I'm not sure you're strong enough to handle a pregnancy. You're going to have to watch everything you eat and curtail all physical activity to just walking," he stated.

169

"I'll do whatever it takes to carry this child to full term, you know that Dr. Thor," Andrea stated.

"I know you'll follow my orders. Now here, take this prescription and have it filled right away. It's for vitamins. I want you to start taking them today," he stated. He started to leave but turned back "One more thing, it's customary for me to see pregnant women once a month until their eighth month, but in your case, I want to see you every two weeks, so make an appointment two weeks from today before you leave."

"Okay," she said as she headed towards the receptionist's desk.

As Andrea returned home, she found Jason waiting for her. He had just gotten home for lunch.

"Hi sweetheart," he said as she walked in the door. "Get all your errands done?"

"Yes, I did," she said as she kissed him. Should I let him know right now that he's going to be a daddy. Maybe, but maybe I should wait until later. Then she looked at the sandwich he was about to eat and she ran straight for the bathroom.

Jason ran after her. "Are you okay?" he asked. "This is the second time today you've gotten sick."

So he had heard her this morning after all.

"I'll be okay in a minute," she managed to say. Jason left her alone.

A half an hour later she came out of the bathroom.

"You look awfully pale. Here, sit down," Jason said as he helped her to the couch. "Maybe you should go see the doctor."

Andrea started to laugh.

"What's so funny?" he asked.

She just couldn't stop laughing.

"Honey, what's so funny about having the flu?" he asked.

She finally managed to get herself under control. "I just came from Dr. Thor's office," she said with a grin on her face a mile wide.

"Well, I hope he gave you something for your stomach. But why didn't you tell me you needed to see the doctor? I would have taken you, you know?" he said.

"I know, but I wanted to go by myself. I wanted to be sure before I said anything to you," she added.

"Be sure? About what?" he asked.

"I wanted to be sure that we were going to be parents before I got your hopes up," she said.

"What! Really! Oh my God!" he said as he gently pulled her into his arms. "I can't believe it!"

"Neither can I," Andrea sang happily.

"What did the doctor say? Is everything all right?" he asked.

"He said everything was just fine, but for me to be very careful. He said that I have to see him every other week so he can watch me carefully. He feels it might be a bit too soon for me to be pregnant after all my body has been through. But I feel wonderful except for being sick to my stomach and that's perfectly normal," she added.

"Let's go tell your parents," Jason said. "They're going to be delighted. I just know it," he continued as they headed for the Higgins house.

After looking through a few rooms, they finally found her parents in the study.

"Hello," Shirley said, "How are you kids today?"

"We're just fine mom," Andrea said.

"Not really," Jason said and Shirley and Tom both looked at him.

"What do you mean?" Tom asked.

"You see, Andrea hasn't been feeling too well for the last couple of days. She went to see Dr. Thor this morning and he said . . ." and Jason stopped.

"He said what for goodness sake?" Tom asked.

Jason looked at Andrea and she mouthed 'go ahead.'

171

"He said that there was nothing to worry about. That five out of every ten women get sick to their stomachs all day long during pregnancy," Jason said smiling. Andrea began to laugh.

"What?' Shirley asked.

"You're going to be grandparents," Andrea said.

"How wonderful!" Shirley added.

"Congratulations!" Tom said shaking Jason's hand and hugging Andrea.

"Did the doctor say everything is all right?" Shirley asked.

"Yup. He just asked me to be extra careful from now on," Andrea said.

"Well, then, I'll just have Marabel send one of the girls over to help you out each day. She can do the cooking and cleaning for you," Shirley stated.

"No, mom," Andrea stated. "I can manage by myself."

"No," Jason said to Andrea. "I think you should accept the help."

"No. It's my house and I enjoy cooking for you now that I've learned how."

"Okay, how about just help with the cleaning and laundry?" Shirley asked.

Andrea looked over at Jason and he was shaking his head in agreement.

"Oh all right," she said. "But only the cleaning and laundry."

Andrea knew there was no way she would win with both Jason and her mother against her.

"Good, it's settled then," Shirley said.

The pregnancy progressed well as Andrea visited Dr. Thor every two weeks. Jason became more and more attentive towards her, and, in their lovemaking, he was more and more intense.

As the weeks passed, Jason watched carefully over Andrea. He didn't want anything to happen to her or the child he wanted so badly.

Soon it was time for the holiday season and Jason hoped to keep Andrea quiet during this time, but he knew it wasn't going to be an easy task. Andrea loved the holidays and she always gave it all she had.

During the next few weeks, Andrea dug into her Christmas shopping, trying to find that special gift for everyone. Jason kept telling her to slow down, but she kept up the pace anyway.

When Christmas Eve finally arrived, Andrea was sure she had gotten everything done and all the appropriate gifts bought.

Our first Christmas together. I never thought this would come true. But here we are she thought. We're actually going to have Christmas together as husband and wife.

Christmas dinner was on Christmas day with her family, but tonight was going to be just the two of them after they attended church services. Andrea so looked forward to their Christmas Eve alone.

When they returned home from church, nearing their front door Jason said to Andrea, "Close your eyes."

"Why?" she asked.

"Just do what I say," he said smiling. She closed her eyes.

"Now, take my hand," as he led her into the house.

"Okay, now you can open your eyes," he said.

Andrea gasped. "Oh Jason, they're beautiful," she said as she looked around the room. All their old furniture had been removed and replaced with beautiful new pieces.

"Oh Jason," was all she was able to say.

"Do you like them?" he asked.

"I love them," she said.

"There's more," he said. "Follow me."

He led her into the room that was to be the nursery and it was filled with baby furniture and a huge stuffed teddy bear sitting in a corner. She turned and hugged Jason very hard as the tears streamed down her face.

"I can't believe it," she said. "Everything is so beautiful! How did you get it all in here?"

"I had some help from some of orchard crew. They put them in here while we were at church," he said.

"Where did you keep it all?" she asked.

"That's a secret," he said. "If I tell you, you'll know where to look next year!"

All of sudden Andrea stopped smiling.

"What's the matter? What's wrong?" he asked.

"It's just that my gifts to you don't come close to these," she said.

"Oh honey," he said as he smiled at her, "I'm sure I'm going to love whatever you got me."

"I don't know about that," she said.

"Well I do," he said, "Let's go open them," and he took her hand and led her back to the living room where she had put all their presents under their Christmas tree.

She watched his eyes as he opened each gift and he did seem to be genuinely pleased with everything she had gotten him.

Then she got up, put some Christmas music on, lit the candles and turned out all the lights except for the lights on the Christmas tree. Jason lit a fire in the fireplace and they snuggled together and lost themselves in their love for each other.

They were up early the next morning and ready to have Christmas with Andrea's family. This year was a very happy Christmas at the Higgins home.

The holiday season for the Higgins family flew by.

As things slowed down after the holiday season, Andrea kept herself busy with preparing the nursery. There was wallpaper to purchase and hang, curtains to be made, and baby clothes to be bought. It was the happiest time for her and Jason as they anxiously awaited her due date, for it was coming closer and closer.

Andrea rose early to get Jason up and out to begin working on the cherry orchards since spring had arrived. After their breakfast, Andrea hurriedly pushed him out the door. Then she sat down to relax a while before cleaning up the morning dishes. Getting up early and fixing breakfast was becoming more and more of a chore, but she wouldn't admit it to anyone. As she sat there she heard a knock on her door.

"Come in," Andrea said. She was sure it would be Sheila, her housekeeper.

"Oh, Sheila," she said, "I would really would like to be alone this morning. Would you please wait until this afternoon to clean for me?"

"Certainly," Sheila said. "I'll be back after lunch." Sheila closed the door behind her as she left.

Andrea sat in her chair and dozed off. She was feeling quite tired most of the time and was having a hard time getting around because she was getting so large.

When she woke, she got up and started to clear the kitchen table when suddenly the room began to spin. Andrea yelled for help as she fell to the floor with a loud crash as the dishes hit the floor with her.

Jason had been quite busy all morning but had decided to head back home a little early for lunch. He liked to look in on Andrea every now and then and he hadn't been able to do it earlier. He kept having a strange feeling that something was wrong at home. He wanted to make sure Andrea was all right.

As he entered the house, all was quiet. He called out, "Andrea are you here?" There was no answer. Maybe she went to see her mother he thought as he headed for the kitchen to get some lunch. As he opened the door, what he saw filled him with terror. There was Andrea lying on the floor, broken dishes all around her and she was lying in a pool of blood.

He quickly went to her, making sure she was still alive and then called for an ambulance. Thank God she was breathing. It took only minutes for the ambulance to arrive, but it seemed like hours. Tom and Shirley were right behind it. They immediately took Andrea to the hospital where Dr. Thor was waiting for them. The ambulance driver had radioed ahead that Andrea was hemorrhaging.

After several hours, Dr. Thor came out to the waiting room to talk with Jason and her parents.

"I'm happy to say that Andrea and her pregnancy are going to be fine. We had quite a struggle for a while, but we managed to save both of them," he said.

Jason sighed with relief. "Can I go see her?" he asked.

"Yes, but stay for only a few minutes. She's quite weak and needs her rest. She's going to have to be here for awhile," Dr. Thor added.

Still, Jason needed to be near her and see for himself that she was all right. He headed straight to her room. As he entered, Andrea slowly opened her eyes.

"Hi darling," she said.

"Don't talk. Just rest," he said.

"Did the doctor tell you everything is going to be all right?" he asked her.

"The baby?" she asked him.

"Yes, even the baby," he said.

"Jason, I was so scared," she said in such a soft voice.

"I know honey. I know. But everything is fine now," he said as he stroked her cheek.

"I love you," Andrea said.

"I love you too," he added.

Then Andrea fell asleep. Jason stayed with her for a while and then left to go talk with her parents.

"Jason," Tom said, "it looks like she's going to have to be here for a couple of weeks and then the doctor said she is to have someone with her around the clock until her time comes to have the baby. Dr. Thor said she isn't to do anything but to eat, sleep, and take very short walks. I told him that Sheila would stay with her while you're at work."

"Why did this happen?" Jason asked.

"The doctor doesn't know," Tom said. "The only thing he said was something about her being so large already and shook his head and then left."

Andrea regained her strength quickly in the hospital and came home at the end of the two weeks. Andrea told Dr. Thor she would do whatever it took to carry her baby to full term and ensure it was going to be healthy. It was obvious she meant what she said. He could tell by the way she was handling her stay in the hospital.

Andrea didn't like having Sheila in the house all day, but managed to adjust to it without much complaining. At least she was company while Jason was working.

After two weeks were up, Andrea went to see Dr. Thor for her checkup. He told her that everything seemed to be coming along fine.

After dinner that evening, Tom and Shirley came to visit and tried to brighten Andrea's blue mood. They knew Andrea was becoming quite bored having to sit around all day. Seeing her parents out the door, they retired for the night.

Sometime in the middle of the night, Andrea woke Jason up.

"Jason," she said as she shook him. "Wake up."

"What . . .what's the matter?" he asked.

"I think I need to go to the hospital," she said.

"Are you sure? You're not due yet?" he asked her.

"I've been awake now for over three hours and I've been timing my contractions. They're three minutes apart now," she replied.

"Good Lord!" Jason said as he jumped out of bed. He dressed quickly and called Dr. Thor. He told them to leave immediately for the hospital, adding that he was afraid something like this was going to happen. Jason wondered what he meant by that, but shrugged it off and went to help Andrea.

Jason carefully helped her out of bed.

"Wait!" she said. "Call mom and dad. Ohh, that hurts," she said as she had another contraction. "They're getting quite strong now."

"If mom and dad wake up and find us gone, they're going to think the worst has happened. I don't want them to be upset," she added.

"Okay, I'll hurry," he said.

He quickly dialed their number, informed them of the situation and then looked at Andrea and said, "Now in the car with you and I'll be right back." Then he ran back into the house to get her overnight case.

Jason sped to the hospital and greeted Dr. Thor who was waiting for them at the entrance to the emergency room.

"Jason, you go get all the paperwork done for admitting her. I'll take care of her now," Dr. Thor said as the nurse placed a name band on Andrea's wrist. Dr. Thor had told them to have things ready for Andrea's arrival so that he could take her directly to the labor and delivery room.

Jason reluctantly let Dr. Thor take Andrea and he headed towards the admitting desk. He returned to the waiting room just as Shirley and Tom arrived.

"Any news?" Tom asked.

"No, not yet. I just got her admitted. Dr. Thor took her right in. I'm going to see her now. That is, if they'll let me," Jason said.

It wasn't long before he came back.

"All seems to be going well with her. They're just now taking her into the delivery room. It shouldn't be long," he said as he nervously sat down.

Andrea didn't have any complications during the delivery. Everything went smoothly. It wasn't long before

Dr. Thor appeared at the door of the waiting room with a strange look on his face.

Jason jumped up.

"What is it? What's wrong? Is Andrea all right?" he asked Dr. Thor.

"Nothing is wrong Jason. Calm down," The doctor said. "Everything went fine. Andrea is just fine. A little tired, but she's fine."

"But what?" Jason couldn't wait any longer.

"Congratulations, Jason," Dr. Thor said looking straight into his eyes, "you are the proud papa of twins. A boy and a girl."

"You're kidding," Jason said falling back on the sofa.

"No, I'm not. I've suspected this for quite some time now, but the ultra-sounds showed only one baby and we could only detect one heartbeat. The babies were perfectly aligned, one on top of the other, and apparently their heartbeats were always in perfect unison. I didn't want to say anything to Andrea about it for fear of how she would react to such news," the doctor replied. "But surprisingly enough, she handled the double birth very well and the news that they are twins of opposite sexes."

"May I go see her?" Jason asked.

"Of course," Dr. Thor said.

Shirley and Tom were astounded. Their little girl had just given birth to twins.

Jason entered Andrea's room. "Hi darling," he said as she smiled at him.

"How's papa doing?" Andrea inquired.

"A little shaky," Jason replied. "When you do things, you certainly don't mess around do you?"

"Nope," she said smiling.

"Have you seen them?" she asked.

"No, not yet. I wanted to see you first," he answered.

"I'll ring for the nurse to bring them in," Andrea said.

As they waited for the twins' arrival, Jason and Andrea held hands. The nurse entered with two

179

bassinets. Jason was at first speechless and could only stare at them.

"They're beautiful," he finally said.

"Want to hold one?" Andrea asked.

"I guess so," Jason replied. The nurse picked up the little girl and handed her to Jason. Then she picked up the boy and handed him to Andrea.

"Have you decided on names yet?" the nurse asked.

"Yes I have," Andrea replied. "What do you think of Alexandria and Alexander?" Andrea asked Jason sheepishly.

Jason slowly smiled and nodded his head in agreement. He understood why she had chosen them.

About the Author

Paula is the author of many technical manuals she wrote during her career. But Paula's dream had always been to write a novel. Outside of her career Paula spent her time raising two wonderful daughters. Now that her daughters have gotten older she has had the time to devote to fulfilling that dream. Paula has always been an avid reader. She believes this has provided her with the insight of what components are necessary to hold a reader's attention and keep them intrigued until the very last page. Over the past few years Paula has taken steps to write her first novel. Paula's wish is that you derive as much pleasure reading this novel as she did writing it.

Printed in the United States
23720LVS00004B/82-510